A SHOT IN THE DARK

Drew limped to the window, pushed it open, and leaned his arms on the sill. Somewhere out there in the warm night, probably watching the hut at this very moment, was the old man who'd turned his life into a living hell.

A sound rustled in the grassy arroyo. Drew knew it was Dayton. He could almost see the tall, thin man with the flopped-down hat squatting in the weeds, waiting for him with the buffalo gun.

Then the moon came out from behind a cloud and everything was as plain as day. There was Dayton—it *had* to be him—his back to Drew, his face obscured by shadow.

"Dayton, you murdering bastard!" Drew shouted, "I've got you now!"

And holding the .45 in both hands, aiming at the dark, motionless figure, he pulled the trigger . . .

VISIT THE WILD WEST
with Zebra Books

SPIRIT WARRIOR (1795, $2.50)
by G. Clifton Wisler
The only settler to survive the savage Indian attack was a little boy. Although raised as a red man, every man was his enemy when the two worlds clashed—but he vowed no man would be his equal.

IRON HEART (1736, $2.25)
by Walt Denver
Orphaned by an Indian raid, Ben vowed he'd never rest until he'd brought death to the Arapahoes. And it wasn't long before they came to fear the rider of vengeance they called . . . *Iron Heart*.

THE DEVIL'S BAND (1903, $2.25)
by Robert McCaig
For Pinkerton detective Justin Lark, the next assignment was the most dangerous of his career. To save his beautiful young client's sisters and brother, he had to face the meanest collection of hardcases he had ever seen.

KANSAS BLOOD (1775, $2.50)
by Jay Mitchell
The Barstow Gang put a bullet in Toby Markham, but they didn't kill him. And when the Barstow's threatened a young girl named Lonnie, Toby was finished with running and ready to start killing.

SAVAGE TRAIL (1594, $2.25)
by James Persak
Bear Paw seemed like a harmless old Indian—until he stole the nine-year-old son of a wealthy rancher. In the weeks of brutal fighting the guns of the White Eyes would clash with the ancient power of the red man.

Available wherever paperbacks are sold, or order direct from the Publisher. Send cover price plus 50¢ per copy for mailing and handling to Zebra Books, Dept. 2016, 475 Park Avenue South, New York, N.Y. 10016. Residents of New York, New Jersey and Pennsylvania must include sales tax. DO NOT SEND CASH.

DAYTON'S REVENGE
BY ERLE ADKINS

ZEBRA BOOKS
KENSINGTON PUBLISHING CORP.

ZEBRA BOOKS

are published by

Kensington Publishing Corp.
475 Park Avenue South
New York, NY 10016

Copyright © 1987 by Erle Adkins

All rights reserved. No part of this book may be reproduced in any form or by any means without the prior written consent of the Publisher, excepting brief quotes used in reviews.

First printing: March 1987

Printed in the United States of America

Chapter I

"I wish you were coming with me," Drew said, smiling down at his wife. Hugging her lightly he bent and kissed her smooth forehead. Then he stepped back, brows raised.

"I do, too" Melissa answered, returning his smile. "But with the way things are expanding, I don't think I should try to make such a long trip from Fort Rather to Tucson."

Lovingly she patted her rounding stomach. "Little Moon, whether a he or she, wouldn't be very comfortable. I hope you're back soon."

"I won't even stop to sleep," Drew said, stroking her pink cheek. "I don't know why Sheriff Judson wants me to come to Tucson right now. I told him all I know about the Indians killing Cap Dayton last year. He should know by now how Slade and Tom were killed."

Melissa pursed her mouth and arched her brows. A twinkle grew in her brown eyes.

"Maybe there was a reward on the Daytons," she suggested, turning her head sideways, "and Sheriff Judson's going to give it to you. We can use it on the baby."

Drew threw back his head and laughter filled the white and yellow living room.

"His telegram didn't mention anything about a reward," he said, putting his arm around her shoulder. He pulled her against his side and they walked to the front door. Looking down at her in concern, Drew narrowed his eyes when he felt a shiver run over her body.

"Are you all right?" he asked anxiously, peering closely into her eyes.

"Yes," she replied slowly, a wan smile turning up the corner of her mouth. "I just got the feeling that something bad is going to happen." Expelling a deep breath she leaned her head against his arm.

"Oh, it's probably just your condition," he soothed, turning her to face him and placing both hands on her shoulders. "Dr. Bryan said you're doing fine, and Mrs. Thrasher is within yelling distance. Little Moon isn't due for another month yet. I should be back even before you know I'm gone."

A bright smile replaced the troubled frown, and she squeezed his arm as they stepped out on the front porch.

"It's too far for you to come to the corral," he said when she started to follow him down the steps. She nodded at his logic. Giving her a long kiss and a gentle pat on her stomach, Drew started kicking through the loose sand in his mocassin boots toward the corral.

"Drew," she called out anxiously after him. He turned around to see her hurrying after him as fast as her ponderous front would allow. Tears were in her eyes when he went back to her. She threw her arms around his waist and held on to him as tightly as she could, her head pressed hard against his chest. His right arm circled around her shoulders; his left hand held her head close against him. "I love you very much," she whispered, looking up at him, her eyes sparkling in the tears.

"I love you more than you know," he replied huskily, raising her chin up to really kiss her. "I've got to go," he said softly, smiling down at her. She nodded, turned slowly, and went back to the house.

Drew Williams saddled a chestnut mare, got a grub sack from the mess hall, and, against his better judgment, led the horse and tied it in front of Colonel Walters's office. The corporal was gone from his desk, so Drew knocked and opened Walters's door.

"Haven't you gone yet?" Walters bellowed when Drew came into the office and sat on a straight-backed chair facing his desk.

Walters was using a white cloth to polish the small gold-rimmed glasses that he hated to wear.

"If I was gone," Drew replied placidly, pushing his flat-crowned hat back, "I wouldn't be sitting here listening to you."

Drew had learned to swap barbs with Walters without any real fear of repercussion. "Did you think of anything else you wanted me to tell Sheriff Judson?" he asked frowning.

A thoughtful frown pulled wrinkles between Walters's brown eyes and his pudgy face seemed to freeze.

"No, I guess not," he finally said, shaking his head. "Just tell him all he wants to know about the Daytons. Wonder why he's so interested in them again? They're all dead." Replacing the glasses, he blinked his eyes. "Oh, well," he said, waving his hand as if dismissing the whole thing from his mind, "you take care of it. You'll know what to do."

Shaking his head slightly and trying to hide a smile, Drew got up, opened the door, and left Walters's office. The corporal had returned and was writing in a ledger.

"Keep a close eye on the old man, will you?" Drew whispered, leaning down close to the young man. "He hasn't been quite the same since Tom Dayton tried to kill me here last year. His nerves were a little rattled by the whole thing."

"I wish I could have been here then," the corporal said enviously, nodding quickly. "I heard about that. Sounds like it was really exciting with all the Indians and a senator, too." Standing up he extended his hand. "Good luck, sir."

The sun had been up for two hours when Drew rode through the log gates of the fort. A lot had happened to him since he'd ridden through that same gate last year. It was a little ironic that this ride was involved with the same people who the first one had been. The situation was so ridiculous that he threw back his head and laughed. The only difference was that it wasn't as hot as it had been then.

His assignment had been to take Melissa Dunbar, daughter of Senator Rance Dunbar, from Fort Rather to Tucson, Arizona. The Dayton brothers, Cap, Tom, and Slade, had sworn they would kidnap her to prevent her father from signing an agreement with Chief Half Moon, in which the Indians would pledge to stop taking guns from the Daytons and raiding wagon trains and settlements, the government in return giving them guns to use only for hunting.

A friend of Senator Dunbar, Charles Sinclair from England, had been along for one day of the three-day trip to Tucson, but his nerves, or lack of nerve, hadn't allowed him to continue — much to Drew's relief.

The Indians had killed Cap Dayton after the brothers captured Melissa and Drew in an abandoned shack. Cap had headed for Tucscon, leaving Melissa and Drew with Tom and Slade. With Melissa's help Drew had escaped and come upon the Indians standing around Cap's body with an arrow in it.

Half Moon and his braves had followed Drew back to the shack where they'd found Melissa guarding Tom and Slade with a gun. The Indians then had taken the Daytons back to Fort Rather so Drew and Melissa could go on to Tucson.

When Drew returned to the fort he had learned that Slade had shot and wounded Chief Half Moon and escaped. Drew had gone after Dayton, found him in a rocky canyon, and killed him with a single shot.

When Drew next returned to the fort he learned Half Moon had decided not to sign the agreement because Dayton had shot him. Walters, in a devious plan, then had promised Half Moon that Drew and Melissa would name their first child after him if he would sign. Half Moon agreed and signed the agreement: as everyone started going about their business a shot was fired — from the guardhouse, where Tom Dayton was being held — that caught Drew in the shoulder. Dayton was killed by the guards, and as far as anyone cared that was the end of the Daytons.

Two weeks later Melissa and Drew had been married. Drew had gone back to leading wagon trains and going on other scouting trips for Colonel Walters. Two months later they'd been happy to learn that Melissa would have a baby at the end of May or beginning of June.

"Life's been so good to me," he said out loud, holding the reins loose in his hands. "Wonder if Little Moon will be a boy or a girl? I hope he or she favors Melissa."

Since the weather was a lot cooler than it had been last July, Drew and the horse were able to cover more ground. Finally stopping by the stream where Melissa had washed the sand-cleaned dishes, he decided to spend the night.

Spreading his blanket on the ground, Drew hobbled the horse near a grassy spot, stretched out on the blanket, and went to sleep.

The first gray streaks of dawn were breaking the horizon when he awoke the next morning, and he knew he could be in Tucson by night if he didn't waste any time. He'd see Sheriff Judson first thing next morning, get the Dayton business cleared up, and be on his way back to Fort Rather before noon. More important, he'd be back with Melissa. He was missing her more than he imagined he would.

When the shack where they'd spent the night came into view as he topped the hill, he allowed himself a few minutes. Dismounting he tied the horse to the small bush, opened the door, and went inside.

If he hadn't known better he'd have sworn that he could still smell the faint fragrance of Melissa's lilac cologne. He shook his head sharply to get rid of the silly idea. Walking slowly around the small room he stopped in front of the log bench where he'd laid Melissa when she'd pretended to faint so she could give him the small derringer from inside her blouse. Something white under the bench caught his eye and he bent down to pick it up.

His heart caught in his chest when he straightened up and unfolded a white handkerchief with a blue M and D stitched in one corner. It must have fallen out of her blouse when she'd handed him the derringer, in their haste to leave the shack afterward both overlooking it.

Drew smiled, folded it into a small square, put it in his left shirt pocket, buttoned the flap, and walked to the door with a backward look. Pulling the door shut behind him, he got on the horse and headed at a fast gallop toward Tucson.

The sun had about two hours to shine when Drew pulled the horse to a stop in front of the sheriff's office. Stepping up on the plank sidewalk he opened the door.

"Where is Sheriff Judson?" Drew asked the deputy who was sitting with his booted feet up on the desk.

"Oh, he's either at the hotel or restaurant," he answered, jerking his feet down, a guilty look on his young tanned face. "There was a shooting at the hotel this morning, and he could be checking that out, or it's almost suppertime and he could be eatin'. If he's not at either of them places, he's probably at home."

At the end of his explanation he took a deep breath.

Wonder what he would have said if I'd asked the time, Drew thought, wanting to laugh.

"Thanks," Drew said, opening the door. "If he comes before I do, tell him I'm in town." Drew wondered at the puzzled look on the young face. "Oh, I'm Drew Williams. The sheriff wanted me to come up here about something that concerns the Dayton brothers."

"Oh, yeah," the deputy answered, nodding quickly. "I will."

Drew left the sheriff's office and was walking toward the hotel when he heard his name called.

"Williams! Drew Williams! Is that you?" The man's voice came from behind him and Drew froze in his tracks. The voice was unfamiliar and he didn't know who or what to expect.

Turning slowly Drew eased his hand down to the Colt .45 strapped low around his lean waist and tied to his muscular thigh.

He couldn't believe his eyes. Standing there was Rick Gregston, a cousin he hadn't seen since the Civil War. Drew, Rick, and the Taylor twins had had the glorified idea that the four of them could take the entire Yankee army by themselves, and they'd all signed up. The twins had been killed two days apart only two weeks later. He and Rick had managed to stay alive, but had gone their separate ways after Lee handed his word to Grant.

"Rick, is that you?" Drew asked incredulously, squinting his eyes. "You old son of a gun! What are you doing here?" The two men shook hands and slapped one another on the back. "You haven't changed much," Drew went on. "You could use a new hat, though." The high oval-crowned hat with a much wider brim than Drew's was cocked to one side on a thick mass of light brown hair that was in complete contrast to the red beard and mustache. The man facing Drew was an inch shorter but had about twenty pounds on him.

"Come on and I'll buy a cup of coffee," Gregston offered, since they were heading toward the restaurant anyway, a grin spreading across his face. "How is Aunt Leet and Uncle Jim?" They entered the restaurant and made their way to a table.

"Mother is still living in Tennessee," Drew replied, pulling out a chair and dropping his lanky frame down on it. "Papa died about five years ago. How about Aunt Sue and Uncle George?" The two men's mothers were sisters.

Before Rick could answer, none other than Sara Judson swept into the restaurant and, as luck or lack of luck would have it, saw them. Surprise and delight brightened her face and she walked quickly toward them. She looked much the same as she had at Dunbar's party. Long red hair was piled up on her head and questioning green eyes sparkled at Drew. The low-cut blue taffeta dress fitted her like a glove.

"Well, Drew Williams," she said in a sultry voice, a seductive smile on her red mouth. "Did you finally get tired of Miss High-and-Mighty Dunbar and come looking for a real woman and something better?"

Her green eyes slid from Drew over to Rick, then back to Drew, and she batted her lashes.

"No," Drew answered, shaking his head slowly while an amused smirk pulled at his mouth. "I won't be tired of Mrs. Williams for a long, long time. The only reason she didn't come with me is we're expecting a baby soon and the trip would be too much for her."

Red color rushed in embarrassment from her neck all the way up to her hair, and Sara Judson spun around on her heel and hurried from the restaurant.

"Something tells me that you and Miss Lashes have met before," Rick said, throwing back his head and laughing loud enough to get the attention of the other restaurant patrons.

"Oh, she and my wife, Melissa, had a run-in last year," Drew answered, a remembering grin spreading across his face. "They tried to pull each other's hair out in a cat fight."

"What were they fighting about?" Rick asked, taking a sip of coffee, a sly twinkle in his eyes.

"In a roundabout way, I guess it was about me," Drew answered, feeling his face turning red.

"You lucky devil," Rick said, laughing again. "I've never had women fight over me."

After they'd drunk two cups of hot coffee and Sam Judson still hadn't come, they left the restaurant and walked down the sidewalk to the hotel. Opening the door and hearing voices coming from the dining room Drew and Rick started toward it. Just as they reached the door Sam Judson came out shaking his head in disgust.

"What's the matter, Sheriff?" Drew asked, stopping in front of Judson. "You look mad enough to bite a rock in half."

"Hello, Williams," he said, looking up in surprise then shaking his head again. "The same old thing.

Two men got into an argument over a card game." Judson pulled his mouth into a thin line. "One said the other was cheating and he shot him. You made good time getting here," Judson went on, extending his hand in greeting. "You must have put wings on your horse." Judson laughed at his own joke and shook Drew's hand.

"Yeah," Drew answered, grinning at the sheriff. "I'm in a hurry to get back to Fort Rather. I'm going to be a father soon and I don't want Melissa left alone too long." Pride swelled his chest out a size bigger. "Oh, this is my cousin Rick Gregston." Drew inclined his head toward Rick.

"He can't be kin to you," Judson argued, shaking his head sadly and extending his hand to Gregston. "He isn't as ugly as you. Let's go back to my office. By the way, congratulations, Williams."

The three men left the hotel and walked back to the jail. As soon as Judson opened the door, the deputy was up from his chair and leaving for supper.

"What do you want to know about the Daytons?" Drew asked as soon as Judson closed the door behind them. "Is this official?"

Judson sat down in the armed chair and tilted it back against the wall.

"In a way it is," he answered pragmatically, pushing his hat back and rubbing his forehead thoughtfully. "A U.S. marshal passed through here about a month ago. He'd heard about the Daytons being dead. Cap was the one he was actually interested in. Seems Cap had killed a sheriff in Lawrence, Kansas, last year. There was a reward out on him. So it's yours."

Bringing the chair back down hard on the wooden

floor he opened the desk drawer, removed a brown envelope, and handed it across the desk to Drew. There was a hundred dollars inside. Drew put the money in a shirt pocket thinking that was a cheap price for a man's life.

"Thanks," Drew said, looking at Judson. There was something about the sheriff that told Drew more was to come. But Judson didn't say anything right away.

"Sheriff, are you telling me everything?" Drew prompted, squinting his eyes. Drew got a questioning look from Gregston. "My gut feeling tells me that there's more to this than meets the eye."

Judson nodded and for a while avoided looking at either man.

"Well," Drew urged irritably, "get on with it. Don't keep us waiting. What else is there?"

"Two weeks ago," Judson began slowly, drawing his lips together in a smacking sound, "an old man rode into town on a mule and began asking questions about the Daytons."

"The Daytons?" Rick interrupted suddenly, a frown pulling his brows together. "Are you talking about the three Dayton brothers?" He jerked his gaze from Judson to Drew. His blue eyes were wide in surprise.

"Yeah," Drew answered, staring at Rick. "Do you know them?"

Gregston was quiet for a second. Then he took and expelled a deep breath.

"I don't know the brothers personally," he answered, drawing his mouth against his teeth. "I've only heard about them. A mean bunch. But I met an old man two weeks ago who rode a mule and who's probably a lot younger than he looks. It's probably the same one you're talking about, Sheriff. He mentioned having three sons who were killed by an army scout." He looked shrewdly at Drew.

"What did this old man want?" Drew asked, looking from Rick to the sheriff.

"He wanted to know who was responsible for Cap Dayton's death," Judson answered slowly. "He said he could understand why and how Tom and Slade died: they didn't have enough sense to get out of the way of a cow. But Cap should have known better. He was the older and a lot smarter and should have found a way out of the mess he was in."

A cold, sick feeling pulled a knot in Drew's stomach. Something told him he wouldn't like the answer to his question.

"Who was this old buzzard and what did he want?" There was an edge in Drew's voice and Judson snapped his eyes a couple of times. Glancing down at the cluttered desk, he slowly raised his head and looked at Drew.

"He said his name was Caleb Dayton," Judson told him slowly. "He said he was on his way to Fort Rather. He had to see somebody there."

"Caleb Dayton," Drew repeated, staring at Judson, then at Rick. "I know I shouldn't ask this, but what relation did he say he was to Cap and the others?"

Sweat that had nothing to do with the heat in the office was beaded on Drew's forehead as he waited for the sheriff's answer.

"He said he was their father," was Judson's slow and solemn reply. "And before you ask, I don't know who he wanted to see at the fort."

Slowly Drew looked from Judson to Rick and back again.

"You don't think . . . ?" Judson let the question trail off. He lowered his head and shook it slowly, then raised his eyes to meet Drew's.

"I don't know what you two are pussyfooting around about," Rick said, cocking an eyebrow and catching his lower lip between his teeth. "But if this old man is the Daytons' father, and if he has an axe to grind against Drew or someone he knows, then we're wasting our time here."

The implication of Rick's words hit Drew with the impact of a board across the stomach. A fear like he'd never known before shortened his breath.

"I think I'd better get back to Fort Rather as soon as possible," Drew said coldly, standing up and adjusting the Colt .45 around his waist. "Rick, do you want to come with me? You'll like Melissa. She's the prettiest thing you'll ever see. Her cooking isn't too bad, either. Colonel Walters will drive you crazy talking about New Orleans, but he's not such a bad sort."

Gregston's mustache and beard twitched as he laughed. "If you hadn't asked me along I was going to invite myself," he said, standing. Removing his hat he smoothed back the thick brown hair and replaced the hat squarely on his head. "Are you ready to go?"

"Yeah," Drew answered shortly, worry in his blue eyes. "I wish I hadn't left so soon. But we should be back in a couple of days. Sheriff," he went on, reaching across the desk to shake hands with the lawman, "if you're ever down our way . . ."

He didn't finish what he was saying, and Judson nodded. They were at the door when a thought struck Drew. "Is Senator Dunbar here in Tucson?" he asked, turning back to face Judson.

"No," Judson answered, tilting the chair back again. "He said he was going to Washington for a few weeks."

Drew and Gregston left the sheriff's office, Drew untied his horse, and the two men hurried on to the livery where Gregston's horse was. Drew waited impatiently as Rick saddled a gray gelding.

"Are you still riding that old bag of bones?" Drew asked in jest. The animal was a good-looking piece of horseflesh.

"You bet," Rick answered, a proud look in his eyes. "I broke Money Man myself, and we've been together for a long time."

Finally they headed south just as the sun was sliding down behind the mountains. Drew knew Rick was right when he insisted that they stop for the night after they'd been riding only for two hours.

"Money Man is fresh," Rick pointed out, reining in the horse under a tree just big enough for a small amount of shade. "Your horse would probably drop in its tracks in two miles. You've been riding him all day."

Clamping his jaw until a knot stood out, Drew expelled a disgusted breath and dismounted.

"I guess you're right," Drew said, undoing the saddle. "If anything was going wrong it would have already happened. You don't actually think that Dayton is out for some kind of revenge, do you?"

In the dim light Rick saw a worried frown pull

Drew's brows together.

"I don't know," Rick answered, swinging down and unsaddling the horse. "But if somebody hurt my family, I'd hunt them until there wasn't a hair left on their head." A cold gleam narrowed Gregston's blue eyes. "Why don't you tell me how all of this happened. We have the time."

Leaning against the saddle and pushing his hat back, Drew started from the time he'd first seen Melissa and Charles Sinclair. The narration took longer than he thought, and when he'd finished total darkness had settled over the land and stars twinkled like diamonds on velvet.

"What do you think?" he asked, squinting his eyes in the darkness trying to see Rick's expression.

"Well," Rick drew out, crossing his long legs at the ankles, "apparently they're a close-knit family. Not for affection, but for survival. That old cur probably raised his pups by the scruff of their necks and thinks he taught them all they needed to know to stay alive. From what Judson said about Dayton being mad because Cap was stupid enough to get himself killed, I'd say he was out to get whoever was smart enough to get Cap."

Rick picked up a dried twig and started chewing on it.

"But I didn't kill Cap Dayton," Drew pointed out. "He was killed by Chief Half Moon's men."

"You know that won't make any difference to a man like Caleb Dayton," Rick argued dryly, shaking his head. "In a roundabout way you were responsible for Cap's death, and his father is looking for you or this Indian. How far is the Indian camp from Fort

Rather?"

"It's only a day's ride," Drew answered, taking a long breath. He hadn't thought about Dayton going after Half Moon. But when the idea struck him he felt a lot better; and he decided he'd try to hold on to that thought until they reached the fort. That would keep Melissa all right in his mind, not that he wanted anything to happen to the Indians.

The two men dropped the Dayton subject and got caught up on family and past activities. They talked well into the night, and finally went to sleep with the sounds of an owl hooting and a coyote's cry breaking the silence. A cool wind blew across the wasteland, and before daybreak both men had to pull up the extra blanket.

Drew opened his eyes just as dawn was dividing the earth from the sky. Rolling to his feet Drew nudged Rick — who was sleeping so soundly that he was snoring — in the side with the toe of his boot.

Even though Drew was in a hurry to get back to Fort Rather, the rumbling noises in his stomach told him that he had to eat something first. Opening the grub sack Drew made flat bread and fried several strips of meat while Rick poured water from the canteens into the well-used coffeepot.

"I never knew that bread and meat could taste so good," Rick said, wolfing down a sandwich. Swallowing the last of the strong black coffee, he saddled the horses while Drew gathered up the bedrolls and tied them on behind the saddles.

"Can we reach Fort Rather tonight?" Rick asked, swinging his leg over the horse's back and settling into a comfortable position on the familiar saddle that had seen many miles.

"We can be there before dark if nothing happens," Drew replied, urging the horse around to head south.

The crisp morning air was cool and the two men let the horses go. They stopped several times to eat and rest the horses. Noon found them by a small stream and a sparse amount of grass.

Rick unsaddled the horses while Drew made coffee, flat bread, opened a tin of beans. Filling the tin plates and cups they sat down in the shade of a cottonwood tree and ate like they had holes in their stomachs.

"By the way," Drew said, reaching over and refilling his cup, "I never asked what you were doing in Tucson. The last time I saw you was when that bluecoat had you in his sights. Luck sure was on your side when his gun jammed. Where did you go after the war?"

A wide grin eased across Rick's face and he shook his head slightly.

"Oh, not long after that I took a bullet in the shoulder, spent a little time in a hospital, and was discharged." Gregston drained his cup and refilled it. "After my shoulder healed I started riding shotgun for Wells Fargo. I'd thought a lot about the Pinkerton Agency but then I changed my mind. I finally got tired of Wells Fargo and decided to go to San Francisco. I was passing through Tucson when I saw you."

Drew threw back his head and roared in laughter.

"San Francisco, my eye," he said slyly, coughing to clear his throat. "You wily devil! I know perfectly well why you want to go to San Francisco. You want to see what the Barbary Coast is all about."

Gregston took a long sip of coffee, threw the rest out, and stood up. There was a gleam in his eyes.

"Well, you're only young and single once," Rick said, slinging the blanket and saddle on the horse. "If you weren't an old married man, you could go with me. We could have a high old time."

Drew got up and saddled his horse, then he and Rick put everything in the grub sack.

An image of Melissa standing on the porch flashed in Drew's mind and he felt a tugging around his heart. But then suddenly a dread tightened his stomach and he felt cold all over. For no apparent reason he remembered the cloud in the sunny sky on the day of the agreement-signing, and wondered if it was a bad omen.

"If you had a beautiful wife like Melissa waiting for you," he said, pulling his hat low to shield his eyes from the sun's bright rays, "you wouldn't care two cents about San Francisco and the Barbary Coast. Just wait until you see her." Drew remembered Caleb Dayton and felt sick. "I only hope you get to see her."

Reaching out, Rick patted Drew on the shoulder. "I'll get to see her," he said with little conviction in his voice. "Don't worry."

The rest of the ride went without incident and Drew had such a mixture of feelings that he was sure he'd smother.

"I've got to let Colonel Walters know I'm back," he told Rick as they rode between the log gates of Fort Rather, "then we'll go on to the house." The sun had three hours before setting. They hadn't wasted any time along the way.

Gregston nodded as he looked around the sprawling fort.

Colonel Walters wasn't in his office, neither was the corporal when Drew opened the door.

"He wasn't in," Drew said, an edge in his voice, swinging up into the saddle. Riding toward the small white house Drew knew instantly that something was wrong. He pulled the horse to such an abrupt stop that its hind legs dug into the sand.

Even though it was early April, the weather was warm enough for the windows and door to be open. Melissa was in the habit of getting up early each morning to make coffee, and if he wasn't going out on a job they'd sit on the porch, drink coffee, and make plans for the future. She would leave the windows and door open so the house wouldn't be so stuffy and hot.

"What's the matter?" Rick asked when Drew pulled on the reins, a frozen expression on his face.

"I don't know, but something's wrong," Drew answered shortly, shaking his head and taking a deep breath.

"How can you tell?" Rick knew from the wild look in Drew's eyes that something terrible had happened.

"The windows are closed," Drew said, leaning over and slamming his heels into the horse's side. The horse lurched forward, and Rick did the same to his horse and was right in Drew's steps when he raced up the steps.

Pausing only momentarily with his hand on the brass knob, Drew pushed the door open and rushed into the living room.

"Melissa," he called out, and waited, then called

again. A frown crossed his face when there was no answer to either call. "That's strange," he continued, coming back from the bedroom.

"Would she visit someone?" Rick asked, watching Drew intently. Drew's face was pale and his eyes were wild.

"No," Drew snapped, then expelled a deep breath and shook his head quickly. "She hasn't been feeling too good lately and tries to rest in the evening when it's this warm."

Pounding footsteps on the porch brought Drew around on his heel, expectation in his blue eyes. Colonel Walters came puffing in, wiping his pudgy face with a big white handkerchief.

"Williams," he wheezed, stuffing the handkerchief back into his pocket, "when did you get back?" His beady eyes darted from Drew over to Rick.

"We just got here," Drew answered sharply. "Where is Melissa? Have you seen her? She should be here." Drew knew he was rambling but couldn't stop. "What are you doing here?"

Walters shifted his gaze from Drew to Rick, then looked down at the multicolored braided rug on the floor.

"I've got some bad news for you, Williams." Walters said slowly, looking up at Drew. "Maybe you'd better sit down."

Before Walters knew what was happening to him, Drew reached out and grabbed him by the front of his white coat and gave him a teeth-rattling shake.

"I don't want to sit down!" Drew yelled, his blue eyes blazing and snapping. "Stop wasting my time! What bad news are you talking about? Where is my wife?"

Drew couldn't seem to stop talking, but he felt the longer he talked the longer he could prevent hearing the inevitable.

"Drew, let him go," Rick said loudly, reaching out and pulling Drew back from Walters.

Walters, sucking in a ragged breath, staggered back and collapsed into a blue and white striped chair. He cleared his throat and looked up at Drew. His face was white and his little beady blue eyes were as wide as they'd ever be. Taking another deep breath he stood up.

"Williams, I'm going to overlook what you just did," Walters wheezed, knowing he was safe from Drew with the other man standing there. "The bad news is—God, I wish I didn't have to tell you this!"

"Tell him," Rick bellowed, taking a step toward Walters, "or I'm going to shake the life out of you myself."

"Melissa is dead." The words were toneless but they bounced off the walls and hit Drew squarely in his being.

He stood like a statue rooted to the floor. The blood in his veins slowly drained away, taking with it all the warmth he knew. In its place was a cold numbness. His lungs were on fire and he realized he was holding his breath.

"Dead?" he repeated, staring at Walters. He shook his head rapidly and squinted his eyes. "How can she be dead? I wasn't gone that long. How did she die? Was it the baby? Is it dead?"

Walters seemed to take forever to answer. But finally he took a deep breath.

"She was killed yesterday morning," Walters said stoically, avoiding Drew's eyes.

"Who did it?" Rick snapped, a deep frown pulling his brows together. "How could she get killed here at the fort with so many people around?"

"I don't know," Walters answered petulantly. "Mrs. Thrasher said she heard Melissa scream around ten o'clock. Knowing about your wife's condition she came running as fast as she could. By the time she got here, your wife was dead. She didn't see anyone. Then she came to get me."

A sick feeling washed over Drew but he had to ask the question. "How was she killed?" He didn't want to know but he had to ask.

"She was shot in the stomach and her throat slit." Walters spit the words out like they tasted bad.

Turning quickly Drew stumbled outside and vomited. When he straightened up, Rick was standing behind him holding a pan of temped water and a yellow towel. Walters stood on the porch, out of the sun, pity all over his pudgy features.

Drew washed his face, stepped up on the porch, and sank down in the rocking chair that Melissa normally used.

"Where is she?" he asked in a hushed breath, then swallowed hard. His voice trembled. "Is she buried yet?" He stared down at the floor, blinking his eyes rapidly. His chin was quivering.

"She's at the doctor's office," Walters said, adjusting the blue campaign hat on his head. Going down the steps he got in the small buggy, popped the reins over the dun mare's back, and drove off.

"Do you want me to go with you?" Rick asked

when Drew stood up and started down the steps. Turning around, Drew looked at him with a dazed expression in his blue eyes.

"Yes," Drew answered tonelessly. The two men got on their horses, rode back to the fort and on to the doctor's office. The last time he had been there was when Dayton shot him in the shoulder at the treaty-signing with Half Moon and Senator Dunbar.

Without knocking, Drew opened the door and Rick followed him inside. Dr. Bryan was sitting at the desk writing in a black book. Hearing the door open he stood up and hurried toward Drew and took hold of his arm.

"Drew," he said softly in his usually gruff voice, shaking his head. "I wish to God this hadn't happened. I don't know what to say." Pain and sympathy were in the old doctor's gray eyes.

"Where is she?" Drew muttered, shaking off the doctor's hand.

"Back here," the doctor answered, leading the way to a side room where patients usually rested. He opened the door and stepped aside so Drew and Rick could go in. The two men removed their hats and Rick took Drew's.

Drew's feet felt like anvils were on them as he moved toward a sheet-covered form on a small bed in the corner of the dim room where the curtains were drawn. His hands were shaking violently as he reached down and picked up the edge of the white sheet.

"Oh, Melissa," Drew moaned out loud when he pulled the sheet away from the still, pale face. The tiny black mole at the side of her nose seemed even blacker. The honey-colored hair lay on her shoulders with several thick curls placed across her throat. Someone had had the forethought to put a light pink dress on her.

"That was her favorite dress," Drew said in a hoarse voice, dropping to his knees beside the bed. He started to pick up her hand but Rick stopped him.

"Drew, don't," Rick said, his hands on Drew's shoulders. "You don't want to remember her like this."

Drew jumped to his feet and pushed Rick away with a violent shove.

"What do you mean, 'like this'?" Drew snapped, his eyes wide and glaring. "She's my wife. She was carrying my baby! Some snake killed her. I've known her longer than I have you, so don't tell me how I want to remember her!"

As Drew turned back around, his gaze fell on a small blanket-wrapped bundle on a table at the end of the bed.

"What's that?" he asked the doctor, turning his head sideways, his face frozen. Dr. Bryan moved over to Drew and put his arm around his shoulder.

"Drew, Melissa was far enough along in her pregnancy that I thought if I could operate on her after she was . . ." The doctor's words trailed off. He shook his head and dropped his gaze. "It was too late. There wasn't enough time. I'm sorry."

Drew hurried over to the table, picked up the light bundle, and cradled it gently in his arms. As tears ran down his checks, he walked slowly back to the bed and laid the baby on the right side of her mother. A rage surged through Drew and he swallowed hard.

"Melissa," he said softly, gripping his hands at his side, "you know I love you and I won't rest until I get Dayton. Little Moon, you would have been as beautiful as your mother."

Then, taking a deep breath, Drew turned, walked past Dr. Bryan, got on the horse, and rode back to the white house.

Chapter II

"Colonel Walters," Drew said in a cold, tired voice. "I'm quitting as army scout until I find Caleb Dayton." He leaned forward in the rocking chair, propped his elbows on his knees, and dropped his chin into his hands. "After . . . ah, after . . . His voice wavered and he cleared his throat. "The funeral . . . I, and Rick if he wants to come with me, are going to go after Dayton."

Walters, sitting in the other rocking chair, mopped his wet and pudgy face with an obviously fresh handkerchief.

"How do you know it was this Caleb Dayton?" he asked skeptically. He didn't want Drew to leave Fort Rather until he retired and went home to New Orleans. Drew was the only one he felt who had enough guts and know-how to get things done to his satisfaction. "Why don't we send for a U. S. marshal and let him find whoever did this?"

Drew couldn't believe Walters had just suggested such a stupid thing. Raising his head Drew glared at Walters and felt a knot working in his jaw.

"Who else could it have been?" Drew asked hotly,

his eyes snapping. "I don't know whether it was just coincidence that Dayton passed through Tucson just when I was up there or if he would've come here while I was at home. I won't know until I catch up with him."

"Until we catch up with Dayton," Rick put in, "or whoever the killer is."

"If we wait around for a marshal to get here," Drew snapped, "we'd only be wasting valuable time. Dayton would be that much further away."

His face was set and Walters knew there was no point in arguing with him. When Williams had his mind made up about something, there was no changing it. There would be no changing it now.

In the short time that Drew and Melissa had been married and lived at the fort, Walters had seen how happy they were. He'd envied the love and closeness the young couple had shared as they awaited the birth of Little Moon. From the cold look in Drew's eyes, Walters pitied Dayton.

"Did anybody come to your office looking for us?" Drew asked, standing up and pushing his hands into his pockets. He should have asked Walters this earlier but had forgotten. Waiting for Walters's answer, Drew felt lost as he looked across the desert to the purple-shrouded mountains. Melissa had thought they looked so peaceful.

"I was gone all yesterday," Walters answered. "Corporal Yates did mention somebody coming by early in the morning."

"Who was it?" Rick asked, without really having to. Drew's head jerked around to look at Walters.

"Yates didn't know," Walters replied, mopping his

face. "All he said was that a dirty old man on a mule come to the office and asked if Drew Williams was still a scout here. Yates sent him to your place." Walters shifted his gaze away from Drew's probing and accusing eyes.

"You didn't hear a shot?" Drew asked, standing up, his eyes riveted on Walters.

"Like I said," Walters whined, "I was gone all day. I—" Drew didn't wait for him to finish what he was saying. Jumping up and stomping into the bedroom, he jerked shirts, two pairs of pants, and socks from the closet, went back into the parlor, took full boxes of shells for the Colt .45 and Winchester rifle, opened the closet and took a yellow slicker that hadn't been used in a long time, and slammed the door behind him.

"What are you going to do?" Walters asked when Drew came outside with his arms full.

"I'm going after Dayton in the morning," Drew replied over his shoulder. Stuffing the clothes in one side of the saddlebag he put the shells in the other side. "Rick and I will spend the night in the barracks. We'll have the . . . ah . . ." His voice choked. He cleared his throat and went on. "We'll have the funeral tomorrow morning and then be on our way."

The two men stood watching Drew, both feeling sorry for him. His hands were working in a frenzy, and he was talking so fast that some of the words were only mumblings.

"Right now, I'm going over to your office and have a talk with Corporal Yates." Without waiting for Rick, Drew swung up into the saddle, kicked the horse viciously in the side, and covered the distance to the office in nothing flat.

"What exactly did the man look like who killed my wife yesterday?" Drew demanded, slamming open the door. The young corporal was so startled that he dropped a bunch of papers.

"Well," he began, taking a deep breath. The cold hard look on Drew's face told him not to waste words. "He was old. Maybe sixty. Tall and thin. Had a red beard, streaked with white. His eyes were a washed-out blue." The corporal stopped to catch his breath. Drew remembered that Cap Dayton had a dirty red beard.

"How was he armed?" Drew snapped, leaning down, his palms flat on the desk.

Once again the corporal was quick and accurate with his answers. "Looked like a Remmington .44 in a holster. Had a knife in a boot sheath and carried a Sharps buffalo gun. Mr. Williams, I'm God-awful sorry about your wife. If I'd know what he was gonna do, I'd have killed him myself." His thin lips began quivering and he dropped his head. "Mrs. Williams was so pretty."

"Nothing we can do now will bring her back," Drew said remorsefully, "or the baby. But he'll live to regret it."

From the cold and deadly expression in Drew's blue eyes, the corporal knew he'd hate to be in the killer's shoes.

"Did he tell you his name?" Drew asked, going toward the door. "Did he say where he was headed?"

The corporal cleared his throat several times and shuffled the papers on the desk.

"He didn't come right out and say who he was,"

Yates replied, "but he did say that he was going to avenge his sons' deaths. He didn't say where he came from or where he was going." He shook his head and slowly met Drew's eyes.

Drew stood, his hands on the doorknob as ideas were gotten and discarded. One idea stuck in his mind and he nodded his head rapidly, drawing his mouth into a thin line.

"Is the chaplain here?" Drew asked, opening the door. When the corporal nodded, Drew stepped out on the porch, closed the door, and wasn't too surprised to find Rick waiting for him.

"What are you going to do now?" Rick asked, walking along beside him. They kicked through the dust as the sun was easing down behind the looming mountains.

Everything was so peaceful and beautiful. Birds sang and an eagle rode the air currents. This time last week, life had been so wonderful. Drew and Melissa had had a great future together. After the baby was born they'd planned to move to Texas, start a ranch, have two more children, and grow old together. All of that was changed now all because some lowlife had taken it upon himself to get back at Drew for doing what he was paid to do.

"I've got to make arrangements with the chaplain for tomorrow," Drew said, leading the way to the white chapel a short distance from the main part of the fort.

"After tomorrow, what are you—I mean, *we*— going to do?" Rick had to lengthen his stride to keep up with the long steps of his cousin.

"We're going after Dayton," Drew answered,

frowning. It should have been more than obvious to Rick what they had to do. Common sense should have told him that.

"I know we're going after Dayton," Rick said, nodding slowly, "but where do we start looking? He has a whole day's start on us, and knows where he's going. We don't."

Rick's inane questions were beginning to get on Drew's nerves. "Why don't you use your head for something besides keeping your ears from slamming together?" Drew asked irritably. As soon as the words were out, he regretted saying them. "Look, Rick. I didn't mean that. I had no right saying it."

Rick slapped him on the shoulder and grinned at him. "Forget it," he said, shrugging his wide shoulders. "If I was in your boots I'd be half crazy. Whatever you decide to do is all right with me."

The chapel was small. Four pews that would probably seat six were on either side of the aisle. A pulpit with a cross carved on it was on a raised platform not far from a small organ.

"Drew, I'm so sorry about your wife and baby," Chaplain Garner said in a deep voice. Drew thought he sounded a little solicitous, but accepted his offered handshake with an obligatory nod. "How can I help you?" the chaplain asked. He bent his tall frame toward Drew and folded his hands before him. His voice and the look in his pale brown eyes were a little more sympathetic than necessary.

"There's no need to postpone the funeral any later than early tomorrow morning," Drew said, getting right to the point. He wasn't prepared for the shocked expression that raised Garner's bushy black brows. The sympathetic look vanished quickly and he frowned.

"Why so early?" Garner asked, pulling at his collar with a long bony finger. "That's unheard of!"

"You're not going to like what I'm about to say, Chaplain." Drew tilted his head to one side and a challenge narrowed his eyes. "Melissa and Little Moon won't be any more dead in the evening than they are right now. The sooner"—he paused and swallowed—"the sooner that's taken care of, the sooner we can go after Dayton."

Garner's thin mouth dropped open in shock and his eyes bulged out.

"Williams, you should be ashamed of yourself!" The chaplain's voice bounced off the walls and rang in Drew's ears. "I pay that God will have mercy on your soul!"

Drew wanted to reach out, grab the black coat, and shake the sanctimonious man gaping at him.

"You'd better pray that God has mercy on Dayton's soul," Drew shot back through clenched teeth, "because I'm going to kill him. Sunrise would be a good time. We'll see you then." His mouth was drawn into a thin line and his eyes snapped.

The last thing left to do was go to the blacksmith's and get a coffin made.

"Won't you be needin' two?" the bear of a man argued when Drew gave him the size of only one. George McKinney stared at him.

"No," Drew refused, shaking his head rapidly. "Little Moon wasn't born. The doctor operated and took her but it was too late. She still belongs with her mother."

Drew's chin began quivering when he saw tears glistening in McKinney's green eyes. He knew if he didn't hurry and get out of this place, he'd break down and cry himself.

"I'll take care of everything," McKinney assured him. "I understand." Drew knew "everything" meant just that.

"She liked that little hill with the cottonwood tree just the east side of the fort," Drew told him. The words stuck in his throat. He turned abruptly and left.

The oval top of the red sun was just sliding down behind the mountains when Drew and Rick left the blacksmith shop and kicked through the dust to the mess hall.

"I'm glad you've finally decided to eat," Rick said, rubbing his stomach. They hadn't eaten anything since early morning. Rick was starving. He was in the habit of having at least two good meals a day, and it was well past eating time. Realizing that Drew was functioning only on nervous energy and grief, Rick hadn't wanted to say anything earlier.

Apparently the troops had already eaten, because the mess hall was empty. A black coffeepot perked away on a potbellied stove, though.

"I'm not hungry," Drew said laconically, taking a tin cup and filling it with strong coffee. "Go in the kitchen and see if Stone has anything left."

Straddling the long log bench, Drew swallowed a mouthful of the hot black coffee. It tasted good. Rick came from the kitchen with a plate piled high with two biscuits, three pieces of fried chicken, and mashed potatoes. His hand moved like a windmill as the food disappeared along with three cups of coffee. Drew couldn't help but smile while he watched the man eat.

Darkness had settled over the fort and desert. This time last week, he and Melissa had sat on the porch, holding hands and talking about Little Moon. He'd never known a man could feel as lonely as he did at this very minute. And guilty.

That was it! That was the strange feeling he'd had ever since he'd gotten back to the fort. Guilt! If he hadn't left for Tucson when he did, he would have been with Melissa when she needed him. It was his fault that he'd lost the best thing that had ever happened to him.

Realizing that sleep wouldn't come easy, Drew knew there was no need to go to the barracks just then. He and Rick climbed the log steps to the catwalk around the fort and looked out across the vastness that was being illuminated by the yellow moon rising in the distance.

"Somewhere out there is a red-bearded old man just waiting for me to come after him," Drew said slowly, leaning against the spike-ended log. "It might take a week, a month, or maybe a year, but I'll get him!"

Drew's face was a mask of hatred in the moonlight. Rick was glad he wasn't the man Drew was after.

The two men stood looking out over the land for a long time. Neither said anything. A coyote bayed at the moon and an owl hooted from a cactus.

"It's my fault, you know," Drew said quietly without looking at Rick, remorse in his voice.

"Your fault?" Rick repeated, spinning around to peer more closely at Drew in the pale light. "What are you talking about? What's your fault?"

Drew didn't answer right away. The words couldn't get past the lump in his throat. He drew back his foot and kicked the wall.

"It's my fault that Melissa and Little Moon are dead," he answered tonelessly. "If I hadn't left for Tucson when I did," he went on slowly, "I'd have been here when Dayton came." He expelled a deep breath.

"You're talking crazy," Rick refuted. "If Dayton meant to get back at you through your family, he'd have done it even if Melissa had been taped under your arm. You've got to stop blaming yourself for what happened and think about getting that lowdown dog!"

Anger edged Rick's voice and he noticed that his hands were gripped in tight fists on top of the fence.

"You're probably right," Drew replied dejectedly. He turned to walk past Rick and started down the steps. "I guess we'd better turn in."

After they'd led the horses to the corral they went to the barracks. Bunks were always available when some of the troops were out. Drew and Rick took the first and second bunks from the wall and stretched out on top of a scratchy blue blanket.

Before long Rick's snoring filled the air. It didn't matter to Drew anyway. Sleep wouldn't come. He tossed and turned. All kind of thoughts raced through his mind.

Which way would Dayton go? Back to Sante Fe. Where had he been before that? Had he been living in the mountains all this time?

This job was going to be a little different from the ones Drew had done before. He'd tracked Indians. He'd guided wagon trains. He'd been caught in sandstorms. He'd survived all of these things and come out with only a few scratches.

Those times he hadn't been personally involved. He'd been paid to do a job, and had done it with no quarter asked. Now he had a duty to do, instead of a job. There would be no pay; just satisfaction and a fulfilled promise.

Drew was glad in a way that sleep was eluding him. If he managed to sleep through the night, he would awake in the morning and he would have to bury Melissa and Little Moon and then start out after Dayton. As long as it was dark, Melissa and Little Moon were only sleeping at the doctor's office.

But God had designed the human body to mend itself no matter what kind of pain it went through. Even though Drew drifted in and out of a dreamless sleep, he did rest some.

In what seemed like a very short time Rick was shaking him awake. At the light touch on his shoulder Drew's eyes popped open and he grabbed Rick's arm. For a second he wasn't sure of his surroundings, then he relaxed his hold on Rick's arm.

"It's almost sunrise, Drew," Rick said in a low voice. Drew sat up, pushed his hair back, and looked around. The troops were getting up and making all kinds of noise.

"Here's a cup of coffee," Rick said, a compassionate look in his blue eyes. Bending down he picked up the tin cup and almost had to force it into Drew's hand. Drew swallowed half of it in two gulps, shook his head, and put the cup down on the floor.

"Let's go," Drew said, pulling on his boots and standing up. Knowing what lay ahead in the next few hours, he felt cold and numb all over. But nothing could stop the inevitable. He and Rick left the barracks, got their horses saddled, and rode outside the fort.

True to the blacksmith's promise everything had been done. McKinney, dressed in dark green pants and a much-too-small green-and-black-dotted shirt, stood beside a wooden coffin, his massive hands clasped behind his back. Garner, the chaplain, displeasure all over his thin face, stood stiffly at the head of the open grave. Colonel Walters looked nervous holding a white hat before him.

A gentle, warm breeze swept across the land, and a few white clouds edged with pink from the rising sun dotted the bright blue sky. This would be a nice day for good things. Not one for a funeral and starting out after a killer. The early-morning hour explained the lack of people, and that's the way Drew wanted it.

"Open it," Drew said softly to McKinney, standing close to the side of the coffin.

"Mr. Williams, please," Garner protested when McKinney bent down and picked up a hammer. "This is unorthodox enough . . ."

Drew used all of his self-control not to reach out and hit the man.

"Open it," Drew repeated, solemnly, kneeling down and glaring up at him. "My wife and child are in there. I'll never see them again and I want it opened." His chest rose and fell in short breaths.

Garner expelled an exasperated breath and pressed his mouth into an irritated thin line. His eyes snapped. His head jerked in a short nod.

McKinney pried the new nails from the lid and slowly eased it off. Drew's breath caught in his throat and his entire body began shaking as he looked down.

"I made you a promise, Melissa," Drew said softly, reaching out and touching her hair. "If it takes forever, I'll do it."

Standing up, he stepped back and nodded to McKinney. The big blacksmith blew his nose on a handkerchief, put it in a back pocket, and tapped the nails in. Then he and Rick picked up the coffin and lowered it into the waiting grave with ropes. Picking up a handful of dirt, Drew sprinkled it on top of the coffin and bowed his head as Garner said a few well-rehearsed words and then, in a monotone, a prayer. Colonel Walters had remained silent all the while.

Before McKinney began shoveling in the dirt, Drew and Rick walked down the hill to their horses. Drew knew he couldn't stand to hear that sound.

"Williams, wait," the colonel bellowed, hurrying after them as fast as his short fat legs could carry him. Drew stopped and waited until Walters caught up with him. Rick went on to the horses.

"Are you really going to leave today?" Walters asked, wheezing with every breath. He'd hoped that after Drew had had a chance to get over the shock of Melissa's and Little Moon's deaths he'd change his mind, stay at the fort, and let a marshal go after Dayton.

"Yeah," Drew snapped, frowning down at the colonel. "Right now, as a matter of fact. After I figure out which way Dayton went, it shouldn't take too long to find him. A mule isn't all that fast, you know." Drew's face was ashen and drawn, but his eyes were alive and snapping with hatred.

Rick was already mounted, and handed Drew the reins to his horse. An odd expression, like there was something more he wanted to tell Drew, crossed the colonel's face and Drew, knowing he'd better ask, did.

"What's wrong?" Drew questioned, one hand on the cantle.

"Ah," Walters began, dropping his gaze to the dry, hard-packed ground, "Charles Sinclair came in on a stage last night. He told me to tell you he wanted to see you after the funeral."

Drew couldn't believe his ears. Charles Sinclair was the last person he wanted to see — or had ever expected to see, for that matter.

"What's he doing here?" Drew asked irritably, a dark frown pulling his brows together.

"Apparently he was still in Tucson when you were there, and he heard about it." Walters answered, shifting his weight from one foot to the other.

"Where is he?" Drew asked, expelling an agitated breath and getting on the horse. Might as well get this over.

"At the same guest quarters he used before," Walters answered, mopping his face.

Muttering an oath under his breath, Drew swung the horse back toward the fort. Rick, judging the look on Drew's face, knew better than to ask any questions.

"This shouldn't take too long," Drew said, dismounting and tying the reins to the hitch rail in front of the small white house.

"Do you want me to come in with you?" Rick asked, still sitting on the horse.

"Yeah," Drew replied, nodding his head. "You might get a lesson in British diplomacy or you might see me cave his head in." He laughed when Rick's brows shot up in surprise.

The two men stepped up on the short porch and the door was jerked open. Sinclair still looked as imposing and pompous as he had when he and Drew had mixed it up in the barracks last year.

"Well, Sinclair," Drew said lightly, cocking an eyebrow. "I never expected to see you again. What brings you down to this barbaric place again?"

Rick got the distinct feeling that Drew was goading this impeccably dressed man. It was all he could do to stifle the laugh building up in his throat. The man standing by the door dressed in light tan flared-hipped pants, a cream-colored shirt, and a white ascot was a sight he'd never seen before.

"Well, really . . ." Sinclair began, then stopped, remembering the first day out on the trip to Tucson. Drew had threatened to ram his riding crop down his throat if he said "really" once more. The humiliation he'd suffered when Drew had beat him up in front of the troops in the barracks had stayed with him for a long time. He clamped his mouth shut and glared at Drew. His brown eyes were threatening.

"You haven't said why you're here, Sinclair," Drew reminded cynically. "We don't have any time to waste, so hurry up and tell me what's on your mind."

So married life hadn't mellowed Williams, Sinclair surmised. He was still as crude as when they'd first met.

"I'll tell you exactly what's on my mind," Sinclair grated sarcastically, his light brown eyes snapping. "I absolutely couldn't believe it when I arrived and learned to my horror that Melissa was dead! I want you to know that I hold you personally responsible for her and the baby's deaths."

The momentary silence filling the room could have been cut with a knife. Drew had never been accused of such a ludicrous thing before and stood mute. But that wasn't so in Rick's case. Sinclair glanced from Drew to Rick and knew instantly that his mouth had gotten him in trouble again. The satisfaction of Drew's stunned silence was short-lived when the ominous-looking stranger took two steps toward him.

"You've got to be the dumbest man alive," Rick roared, reaching out his big hands toward Sinclair's throat. "How could Drew be responsible for his wife's death?"

The color drained from the Englishman's face and his eyes almost fell out of their sockets. Stumbling backward, he fell against the wall. That was all that kept him from landing on the floor.

"Wait, Rick," Drew said slowly. "He has a right to say what's on his mind, and besides, I want to hear it." He looked back at Sinclair and wanted to laugh. Sinclair was breathing hard and his usually plastered black hair was hanging down in his eyes. "All right, Sinclair, let's have it." Drew wasn't aware of it, but his right hand had dropped to the handle of the Colt .45 tied low on his leg.

"Well, I . . ." Sinclair stammered, noticing the gesture, unsure if it was intentional or an accident.

"If Melissa hadn't married you she'd still be alive right now! If you hadn't gone off and left her she'd be alive right now! I should have made her stay in Tucson. She'd be alive right now!"

Suddenly it dawned on Sinclair what he'd said. It hit Drew at about the same time. The men's eyes locked and they stared at each other for a second. Gregston picked up on it also.

"Well, then," Rick accused in a flat voice, "you can blame yourself as much as Drew." He started toward Sinclair again and once more the color that had begun creeping up the Englishman's face drained away.

"Neither of us is to blame," Drew said softly although he knew he'd feel the guilt for a long time. "It was one of those things that happened—but Dayton will pay for it."

Sinclair was a hard man to teach the lesson of keeping silent. "How will he pay for it?" he asked wearily, feeling better after Drew had admitted that there was some guilt on his part. "I guess you're going to stand there and tell me you're going after him by yourself. Or are you taking along a bodyguard?" He nodded his head toward Rick. His lips curled back in a sneer and his eyes narrowed.

Drew hadn't liked Sinclair from the first time he'd seen the man. He tolerated him more or less because of Melissa. But after Sinclair had abandoned them in the desert and then instigated the fight in the barracks, Drew had lost all respect for him. Now he was questioning Drew's ability to go after Dayton alone. Sinclair's remark rankled Drew to the core, and he could feel the short hairs stand up straight on the back of his neck.

"No, I don't need a bodyguard, Sinclair," Drew answered tightly, his jaw working. "If you don't have anything else to say, we've got a lot to do and a long way to go." Drew and Rick started toward the door.

"Well, really," Sinclair blurted out in disgust. "What's the matter with you? Melissa was buried only a short while ago and you can't wait to get away."

Before Drew could think his left hand shot out and grabbed Sinclair by the front of his cream-colored shirt and jerked him forward. Drawing back his right fist he smashed it into the center of Sinclair's face. Drew felt the bone break in Sinclair's nose as blood spurted out and ran down into his mouth and chin.

"Now I can go with a clear conscience," Drew said, spitting out the words and flexing his hand. When he let go of Sinclair's shirt, there was nothing to hold the Englishman up and he crumpled to the floor in a bloody heap. "Let's go, Rick."

Getting on their horses Drew and Rick rode out of the fort. Drew could feel Rick's eyes on him and he wanted to laugh. If Rick didn't say something soon he'd burst.

"Go ahead. Say it," Drew urged, turning his head slowly. This time he couldn't repress the laugh. Rick's mouth was hanging open and his eyes were wide in dismay.

"You could have killed that fool," Rick blurted out, pushing back his hat and shaking his head.

"He deserved it and more," Drew said sharply, taking a deep breath. "He's the type of person who talks big and does little."

Rick didn't question Drew when he turned his horse toward the hill again. They stopped for only a few minutes. Removing his hat Drew bowed his head. Rick saw his mouth moving, but wasn't sure if he was praying or saying a silent good-bye to his wife and child.

After Drew had taken a deep breath, expelled it, blinked his eyes a couple of times, and swallowed, he nodded, kneed the horse in the side, and he and Rick were on their way. One was sure he'd never pass this way again. The other not so sure.

They were quiet as they rode along while Drew worked at pulling himself together. If he'd been told last week that by now he'd be without a family and would have beat up Charles Sinclair again, he'd have called them a raving lunatic.

But all of that had actually happened. The only good about the whole thing was being in the company of a cousin he hadn't seen in a long time. He might come in handy, and his presence would help pass the time.

"Well," Drew said. He expelled a long breath and looked up at the blue sky, adjusted his hat lower on his forehead. "Where do you think we should start looking for Dayton?"

"I was just going to ask you the same thing," Rick replied, relieved that Drew was trying to at least put the saddest part of his life in the back of his mind for a while and concentrate on finding Dayton. "You should know more about the habits of a hider than I do. Where did the Dayton boys hang out when they were in the hide business?"

Thoughtful for a minute, Drew sucked his lips in

against his teeth. "Oh, they were all over the place," he answered complacently, relaxing his grip on the reins. "Chief Half Moon and his people have been moving around for a few years and I guess the Daytons stayed pretty close to them. Hey," he shouted, jerking around in the saddle to face Rick. "That's it. Maybe Half Moon or some of his people could have seen Dayton. His camp is about three miles over that hill and in a valley. Why don't we go ask him?"

Drew laughed when a wide-eyed and open-mouthed gasp burst from Rick's throat and the color drained from his face.

"What's the matter?" Drew asked, trying to hold his face straight. "Haven't you ever seen an Indian?"

Rick swallowed a couple of times before answering. "Well, not eyeball to eyeball. Wells Fargo riders didn't have much reason to call on Indians, you know. But maybe he can help you since you and—" He clamped his mouth shut to bite off Melissa's name. Drew was doing okay and he didn't want to ruin things now. "Since you know him so well."

The smile stayed on Drew's brown face, but Rick saw his eyes blink and knew he hadn't missed the slip.

"I promise not to let any of Half Moon's men take that mop of hair," Drew said, reaching over and socking Rick on the shoulder.

A black yapping dog met the two men as they reached the sprawling camp of teepees. Most of the braves knew Drew and did nothing to stop them as they rode to the largest teepee in the center of the camp.

Half Moon must have heard the racket and the

horses approaching, because he threw back the flap and came out to meet them. The solemn expression in his black eyes told Drew that he'd heard about Melissa and Little Moon.

"Get down," Half Moon invited kindly. "We talk." He pointed toward the teepee. The three men went inside and sat down on blankets placed around a small fire. As was Drew's nature he got right to the point after he'd introduced Rick to the chief.

"Have you or any of your men seen an old man riding a mule in the past few days? He wears . . ." Drew stopped and turned to Rick. "You said you saw Dayton a few days before I got to Tucson. You tell Half Moon what he looks like."

Rick, sitting eyeball to eyeball with his first Indian, didn't really know how to start. He hesitated until Drew cleared his throat meaningfully. Taking a deep breath to relax, and realizing that Half Moon wasn't going to bite him, Rick smiled.

"The man I saw was tall and thin," Rick said, squinting his eyes. "He wore a floppy black hat, a long black coat, and knee boots. He carried a Sharps .54 rifle." Pausing to think if he'd forgotten anything, Rick snapped his fingers. "Oh, yeah, he rode a mule."

Half Moon glanced from Rick over to Drew and shook his head slightly, the black braids moving only a little.

"Why you not say mule in first place?" Half Moon questioned solemnly. From the few times Drew had seen Half Moon he knew the chief was irritated with Rick, but he would probably have done the same thing if he'd been in Rick's boots.

"Why?" Drew asked, leaning forward and peering

closely at the dark-skinned man across the fire from him. "Have you seen him?"

Half Moon nodded but said nothing. It was all Drew could do to keep from reaching out to shake the stolid figure sitting there. "When? How long ago?"

A thoughtful expression squinted the narrow eyes and Half Moon pursed his mouth slightly. Drew was almost at the end of his patience, but he knew better than to try and hurry the Indian.

"Two suns ago," Half Moon finally said, bringing his gaze to meet Drew's. "Standing Bear saw man like that. Not see many white men ride mule. Why you want to know?"

Drew couldn't speak for a minute. Dropping his head he stared at the red coals in the rock circle on the ground.

"The old man is Caleb Dayton," he finally said, taking a deep breath. A knot worked in his lean jaw. "He's the father of the three Dayton brothers who used to give you guns."

Drew's voice was edged with disgust and irritation and he didn't try to hide it. Both Rick and Half Moon noticed it. The Indian dropped his head a fraction.

"I'm not sure if he knew that I was away from the fort or if it was just coincidence," Drew said, meeting Half Moon's eyes. "Maybe it would have happened if I'd been there. Anyway, he killed Melissa and caused the death of Little Moon. A little girl. She would have looked like her mother."

Genuine shock popped open Half Moon's eyes and his bronze skin lost a degree of color.

"Why?" Half Moon's question hit Drew like a slap

in the face, bringing home the real reason he was after Dayton.

"Because he wanted to get back at me for killing Tom and Slade," Drew answered bitterly. The names left a nasty taste in Drew's mouth and he felt sick.

"You think he come after me?" Half Moon asked, his eyes squinting in a frown. "You not kill Cap Dayton. My brave did."

"I don't know," Drew answered, shrugging his shoulders and shaking his head.

"Which way was he going when Standing Bear saw him?" Rick asked, getting to his feet. They'd wasted enough time here, to his way of thinking, and he was ready to get on with the business of finding Dayton.

"He was going toward the east," Half Moon answered, getting quickly to his feet. "If he was after me, he would have come already. No. Not me." He shook his head, a small smile on his thin lips.

Drew stood up, a thoughtful frown pulling his brows together. Rick noticed the look.

"What's on your mind?" Rick asked him when they were outside in the warm sun.

"Since Dayton accomplished what he set out to do," Drew answered, squinting his eyes against the glare, "why would he go east? That would take him to New Mexico or Texas. There aren't that many buffalo in those states. Why wouldn't he head back to Wyoming, Montana, or the Dakotas? That's what I'd do."

As Drew and Rick left the Indian camp, something in the back of Drew's mind told him that things weren't right. Why would Dayton go to a part of the country where there was nothing for him? It didn't make any sense. Maybe that's what Dayton wanted him to think.

Hunger pains and the midday sun found them by a clear stream. Dismounting, Rick led the horses to the stream to drink while Drew filled the coffeepot. Drew made flat bread, then opened a can of beans and dumped them in the hot skillet after the bread was done. When they'd eaten, there wasn't a crumb of bread or one bean left. Each man had had two cups of steaming black coffee and the pot was drained.

While Drew was putting the cleaned utensils back into the grub sack, a thought hit him like a streak of lightning.

"Dayton wants us to think he's heading east," Drew said, one hand holding the reins, the other on the cantle. "He made sure someone would see him, tell me, and I would start out on some wild ride after him."

Swinging up in the saddle Rick stared at Drew, wondering what he meant. If Dayton had been seen riding east, why would Drew think otherwise?

"You don't break an old hider's ways," Drew said shrewdly, pursing his lips and shaking his head slowly. "I don't think he'll go after Half Moon just yet. If I'm guessing right about what he's thinking right now, he figures I'm off to nowhere, and that I'll ride so far away, I'll never catch up with him and I'll give up when I don't find him. He has no way of knowing you're with me."

Pulling the horse to a stop, Drew stared down at the saddle horn. Rick could almost see the wheels spinning in Drew's head.

"What are you going to do?" Rick asked, taking a blue handkerchief from his pocket. He wiped the rolling sweat from his face, removed the black hat, cleaned the sweatband, and replaced the hat, all the while watching Drew.

"We're going to turn back north here," Drew said, a satisfied and determined look in his blue eyes. "Dayton is so far ahead of us that he's in no hurry. He could stop several times to see if his plan is working."

All of this sounded silly to Rick. If Dayton was so far ahead of them, why would he waste his time stopping? He could feel a frown on his face. Drew's eyes narrowed when he looked at him.

"You think I'm crazy, don't you?" Drew asked coldly.

"No," Rick replied slowly. "You've tracked people before, so I guess you know what you're doing." There was skepticism in his voice.

Hot rage burst through Drew's body. Gregston had his nerve! Here he was, along more or less for the ride, and he was questioning Drew's ability and intentions, if only in a roundabout way. He sounded a little like Charles Sinclair.

"Let me tell you something right now," Drew snapped hotly, his eyes blue ice. "If you don't like the way I'm handling things, you have four directions to go. I know how Dayton's thinking. I know what he's doing. I can get him if I work alone. We can get him if we work together. I don't mind having you along, but it's got to be my way!"

Rick was surprised at Drew's temper, and thought grimly about what would happen when he caught up with Dayton. But he had the gut feeling that Drew would need him before this thing was over.

"Okay," Rick said, a grin pulling at his mouth.

"We'll do it your way." Then, "I didn't know he could get so mad," he said under his breath. He didn't mean for Drew to hear that, but he did. They both laughed after some of the tightness went out of Drew.

Chapter III

Drew pushed the altercation with Rick far back into his mind. He realized that this was probably Rick's first time out on something like this and was well within his right to question him. Rick could end up getting killed. Thinking about it in a calmer attitude, Drew knew he would probably have done the same thing.

Believing now that Dayton would head back north, Drew and Rick rode even after the golden rays of sunset had turned into darkness and settled over the land.

They had stopped several times to rest the horses and snack on jerky, but finding a suitable place to spend the night they unsaddled the horses, spread out the blankets, and once again filled their stomachs with bread, salt pork, and coffee. Rummaging through the grub sack Drew was pleasantly surprised to find a tin of peaches, which didn't last very long. They even sopped up the juice with bread.

A pain ripped through Drew's chest and heart when he gathered up the dishes and cleaned them with sand. Remaining in the squatting position until the feeling passed, he stood up and allowed a soft smile to pull up the corners of his mouth.

"Is something wrong?" Rick asked, kicking sand on the red coals. He knew Drew was thinking of either Melissa or Dayton.

"I was just remembering what a fit Melissa had when she saw me clean the dishes with sand when I was taking her to Tucson."

His voice was barely above a whisper and Rick had to strain to hear him. Not knowing how Drew would react to rekindled memories, Rick didn't say anything for a while. When he did, he decided to play it safe and say something about Dayton.

"How far ahead of us do you think Dayton is?" As soon as he'd asked the question Rick wished he could bite his tongue off. To mention Dayton only brought to mind why they were out here in the first place.

"Not too far," Drew answered slowly, expelling a deep breath and stretching out on the blanket, "even though he's had enough time to be back in Tucson by now."

Cold chills ran up and down Drew's back and he shivered even though it was still very warm.

"You don't think he's hiding behind a cactus watching us, do you?" Rick asked. Something in his voice made Drew want to laugh.

"Could be," Drew answered with a cough. Just before he pulled his hat down over his eyes he glanced over at Rick. He was amused at the worried expression on his cousin's face. "You aren't afraid, are you?"

"No," Rick snapped and then was quiet.

Sleep soon closed Drew's eyes and the last thing he heard was the crickets singing and a whippoorwill in a nearby tree. Rick's snoring almost drowned out the sounds. A cool, gentle wind blew over the land.

The sound seemed to come from nowhere and everywhere all at the same time. For a split second Drew wasn't sure whether he was still sleeping and having a dream or was wide awake and actually hearing the eerie sound.

Easing up on his left elbow he pulled the Colt .45 from the holster and listened intently. He was awake; the sound came again, so it had to be real. Rick was wide awake when Drew glanced at him but he was lying perfectly still. Just as Drew was about to say something to him, the sound came again.

"Williams, ye ain't through payin' yet. There's more to come. But ye won't know when or where it'll be."

It dawned on Drew that he was hearing a voice. It sounded raspy and like it came from a rusty barrel. The words were slow and deliberate so there would be no mistake in the meaning.

Thinking that the sound was coming from behind him Drew jumped to his feet just as Rick did.

"Who in the devil is that?" Rick asked in a whisper.

"It's Dayton," Drew answered quietly. "But I can't tell where he is. Can you?" In the moonlight Drew saw Rick shake his head.

They waited for what seemed a long time. But everything was quiet. Even the crickets had hushed. The only sound was the endless wind.

"Are we going after him?" Rick asked, easing over to Drew. From the tone in his voice he was scared, but no more so than Drew.

"No," Drew replied, shoving the pistol roughly back down in the holster. "Not tonight. If Dayton's smart enough to get this close without us hearing him until he started talking, we'd never be able to find him in the dark."

They stood listening again. There was nothing to hear. Nothing except the wind and other usual desert noises.

"You're probably right," Rick said, expelling a deep breath. "Do you think one of us should stand guard while the other sleeps?"

Drew's boisterous and uncontrollable laughter echoed across the land. "Are you kidding?" he finally asked, clearing his throat and slapping his hands against his legs. "Dayton could have killed us while we were sleeping. Unless we get lucky in the morning and find his tracks, we won't see Dayton until he wants us to."

Taking assurance in his own words, Drew went back to his blanket and sat down. Rick walked slowly over to his blanket but continued standing.

"Are you going to sleep like that?" Drew asked, squinting up at him. It was hard to see in the waning moonlight.

"No, I guess not," Rick replied, dropping down on the ground and expelling a deep breath. "But something tells me that I won't get much sleep."

"You'd better," Drew advised, stretching out and resting his head on the saddle. "Something tells me that we're going to use a lot of energy tomorrow, so you'd better sleep while you can."

The last thing Drew remembered before sleep closed his eyes was hearing Rick thrashing around on his blanket.

Gray streaks of dawn were breaking the horizon when Drew opened his eyes the next morning. He wasn't surprised to see Rick already up and making coffee.

"We might as well eat before starting after Dayton," Rick explained, seeing the questioning look in Drew's eyes. Drew hurried to slice meat while Rick stirred flour, salt, and water together for flat bread. After wolfing down the meal they threw the things together, saddled the horses, and began a slow but widening circle to see where Dayton's tracks would lead.

The circle expanded to almost two hundred yards and they still hadn't found any kind of tracks, human or animal.

"Dayton must be carrying that mule," Drew called out as he rode toward Rick, "and Dayton has to be floating. In all of my tracking jobs there's usually been some telltale signs. Other than that voice last night, it's as if he never was here." Drew's brows pulled together in a tight frown. He pushed back his hat and thoughtfully rubbed his thumb across his forehead.

"What are you thinking?" Rick asked, watching him.

"If what I'm thinking is true," Drew said, squinting his eyes and chewing on his underlip, "Caleb Dayton just made a liar out of me in knowing all about tracking. Let's ride back to where we camped."

Rick didn't know what Drew had in mind, and he would have been surprised if he knew that Drew didn't have an idea either. Drew was just going on gut instinct.

Back at the campsite Drew dismounted and sat on the hard ground in much the same way he had last night. Rick stayed on the horse, frowning down at him.

"Dayton's voice seemed to be coming from all around us last night," Drew said, closing his eyes. "But thinking about it now, his voice really sounded like it was coming from the south."

"The south?" Rick repeated, surprise raising his brows. "But that wouldn't take him back up to buffalo country. South of here is . . ." A look froze on his face and he stared down at Drew.

Drew opened his eyes and slowly raised his head to look up at Rick and nod.

"Mexico," Drew finished, a tight smile pulling his mouth in against his teeth. "That sly old devil pulled the wool over our eyes — or mine, anyway. He figured I'd head north after him. He'd hide out in Mexico for a while and then come after me."

A cold, set look glazed Drew's blue eyes and a knot worked in his jaw. Jumping up from the ground he swung up in the saddle, jerked the horse around, and he and Rick started out in a fast gallop almost in the same direction they'd just come from.

Winding in and out of the rocks and cactus Drew got the feeling they were being watched, but something told him that it was only Indians.

Drew hated to admit to himself that he'd been wrong about Dayton, and felt bad that he'd lost his temper and jumped on Rick yesterday. The old man was apparently smarter than his three dead sons. Knowing he owed Rick an apology, it galled him to have to do it. Melissa was the only one he'd ever apologized to, and that was when he'd inadvertently hurt her feelings and made her cry. Now would be as good a time as any to do it and get it over.

"Rick," he began slowly, dropping his head, "about yesterday, I—"

"Forget it," Rick interrupted, reaching over and punching him on his shoulder. "I thought he'd go north, too."

The galloping ride was easy on both men and horses, and the miles passed quickly under the shod hoofs. Stopping several times to rest both themselves and the horses, they rode until the afternoon sun found them on the outskirts of Nogales, Mexico. That was the closest town of any size where Dayton was likely to be.

"He'll probably head for the nearest saloon," Drew predicted, tying the horse to the hitch rail in front of a small, nondescript building with "Try Your Luck" painted over the sagging door in red paint. Kicking through the powdery dry dust, he and Rick pushed open the batwings and stepped into a crowded low-ceilinged room. The inside didn't look much better than the outside. The bar, with apparent bullet holes in the front, was centered, with just enough room to walk behind it, against the wall.

Bottles and glasses were stacked on the corner at the edge of the bar. Six card tables, a roulette wheel, and a rickety piano made up the meager furnishings of the establishment. Lamps suspended on chains from the bare rafters and body heat made it stifling hot and sweat popped out on Drew's face.

"Do you see anybody who looks like the man you saw in Tucson?" he asked Rick loudly. Voices and random music made conversation almost impossible.

Drew watched Rick slowly move his gaze around

the room. There were only four Mexicans in the saloon, and they sat discreetly in a corner. Rick quickly moved his gaze past them and on to the six white men there. After a few seconds he shook his head.

"Nope," he said, turning toward the door. "He's not here. And I don't blame him. I wouldn't drink anything out of those glasses. Do you see how dirty they are? A roach wouldn't be caught dead in this place." The batwings flapped shut behind them.

"Wonder how many saloons there are in Nogales?" Drew asked, looking up and down the street. Then he answered his own question. "There should be at least one more that's a little better than that one." He shivered, thinking about a dirty roach crawling around in a glass he would drink from.

A young Mexican boy came skipping down the street, kicking a short piece of wood before him. Undoubtedly he knew most of the people in town, because he called three white men by name as he passed them and they waved at him. As soon as his dark brown eyes spotted Drew and Rick he rushed toward them.

"Peso, gringo," he said, holding out a grubby brown hand, hopeful expectation shining in his eyes.

"Sure, why not," Drew said, smiling down at the tousled-black-haired boy in a once-white shirt and light tan pants. Reaching into his pocket, Drew pulled out a dollar and held it out to the boy. "But first you've got to earn it. Okay?"

The boy's eyes got bigger when he saw the money, and he nodded his head rapidly.

"Okay," he agreed, a wide smile showing white

teeth. "I earn peso doing what?"

Drew flipped the shiny coin in the air, and the boy's hand darted out and up and he snatched the dollar in one swift downward motion.

"We just need some quick information," Drew said, hooking his thumbs on his pockets. "How many saloons are there in town? I don't mean this one," he said, chuckling, when the boy pointed to Try Your Luck behind them.

The boy ducked his head and grinned sheepishly. Then he raised his head and an angel couldn't have looked as innocent.

"Only two more, gringo," he said and paused, a slyness in his eyes. Hesitantly he held out his dirty hand again.

"Two names for two dollars isn't bad, Drew," Rick said, throwing back his head and laughing. "It would save a lot of looking."

"I guess you're right," Drew said, reaching back into his pocket and pulling out two more coins. The boy swept them out of his hand with a motion too swift for the eye to follow. Drew wondered how many other "gringos" had been bilked by this enterprising youngster.

"Okay," Drew said, cocking an eyebrow and trying to look stern, "where are these expensive saloons?"

Turning around the boy extended his arms and pointed to both sides of the street.

"Noche de Oro is halfway down that side"—the boy pointed to the left—"and Placio de Plesur is at the end of the street." He pointed to the right. His eyes brightened and he rolled them up. "Placio de Plesur is *mucho bueno*, gringo." He smiled slyly.

"How do you know what goes on in there?" Drew asked, a mock glare in his eyes. "You're too young to go into a place like that."

The boy grinned and dropped his head a little. "I don't go in señor," he replied, raising his head and smiling. "There are peepholes."

"Thanks for the information," Drew said, laughing and reaching down to tousle the mop of black hair. "I'm glad there weren't any more saloons in town," Drew said after the boy ran down the street.

"Do we split up or stay together?" Rick asked when they began walking down the dusty street.

"We should stay together since I don't know what Dayton really looks like," Drew said, reaching down and loosening the pistol in the holster. He had the idea that Rick didn't want to split up, anyway.

Noche de Oro was in complete contrast to Try Your Luck. The low, wide building was adobe with red cobblestone roof. Four arched windows let music from a guitar, violin, and accordian out, and the batwings were wide enough to allow two big men to go in and out at the same time.

Chills of apprehension ran up and down Drew's back and his stomach tightened into a knot. He imagined the hairs on the back of his neck were standing out like flags. A gut feeling told him that something was going to happen in this very place.

Drew pushed open the batwings on their well-oiled hinges and Rick followed him in, right on his heels. The clientele was definitely opposite that of Try Your Luck. The patrons in the first place had been a scrappy-looking bunch of men. But those here were better dressed, and subsequently, drinking a better vintage of beer and whiskey out of very clean glasses.

A mahogany bar ran the length of the room. Various-sized bottles with amber-colored liquid and sparkling clean glasses were stacked in neat rows under a gilded mirror. At the far end of the saloon, a black-haired Mexican girl was doing a firy dance, swishing a yellow and black tiered skirt and stomping her feet in a staccato rhythm with the guitar.

Moving up to the bar, Drew and Rick ordered a beer and watched the girl finish her dance. The guitar player struck the strings furiously, the girl slung her head back, snapped the black castanets twice, and her dance ended. Thunderous applause and whistles erupted, and the girl turned and gave the patrons a wide, red-lipped smile.

"Now, that's a good-looking woman," Rick said in a whisper, taking a long pull from the beer. "Wonder what her name is?"

Drew looked around at Rick and wanted to laugh. Rich was almost drooling. There was a mesmerized expression in his eyes.

"Why don't you ask her?" Drew suggested, coughing and clearing his throat. "Here she comes."

"*Buenos noches, gringos*," she said in a sultry voice, dabbing her damp face with a white handkerchief pulled from the low-cut black bodice. "Want to buy me a drink?"

Her liquid black eyes ran over Drew with more invitation then any man was entitled to. But Drew didn't want any involvement right then. He stepped aside and pushed her in beside Rick. The expression didn't change in her eyes, and Drew guessed that Rick looked as good to her as he had.

"What's your name, beautiful?" Rick asked, his blue eyes traveling up and down her curvy figure. "What are you drinking?"

"I am Annaletha Zuniga," she purred, batting her long lashes up at him, slipping her arm through his, "and I would like a glass of champagne."

The mesmerized look froze on Rick's face and then a slow grin tugged at his mustache. He figured he could afford at least one glass of the stuff. A girl who looked that way was worth the price.

"Sure," he said, shrugging his shoulders, "why not. Barkeep, give the lady a glass of that bubbly stuff."

The white-shirted Mexican bartender hesitated at first, and if Rick had been paying any attention he would have seen a little fear in his black eyes. But he poured a light-colored beverage into a long-stemmed shallow-bowled glass and handed it to the smiling woman at Rick's side.

Drew knew this was only a passing thing for Rick, but he also knew how Rick thought he felt. Drew was positive he'd had the same kind of look on his face when he'd first seen Melissa. For a second he allowed himself a few memories, but was jarred out of them when the batwings slammed open and shut and he thought a herd of cows was coming at them, from the noise of feet and voices. He had just enough time to turn his head toward Rick when he saw two massive brown hands clamp down on Rick's shoulders and spin him around.

Oh, my God, Drew thought, rolling his eyes toward the ceiling and taking a deep breath. He eased the beer mug, with only one sip taken from it, down on the bar.

The huge Mexican grinning a cold threat down at Rick would almost make two of him. Thick black curly hair covered his head like a woolly rag. Sideburns reached down the side of his wide jaws. Straight black brows hooded deepset dark brown eyes. Singletree-wide shoulders were covered with a dazzling white shirt opened halfway down the front, revealing a barrel chest covered with a mat of black hair. A silver chain with a cross glittered around the massive neck. Black flare-legged pants, with silver conchos down the side, encased thick legs. The man reminded Drew of a bear he'd seen once on a hunting trip up in the high country. That's where Drew wished he was right then.

"Heeee, gringo," he said, a fake lilt in his deep voice. His mouth under a thick mustache pulled to one side in a slow grin. "You are talking to the wrong woman. Annaletha belongs to me and nobody talks to her except me. Comprende?"

Tilting his head to one side and arching his brows he gazed down at Rick.

All the color had drained from Rick's face and his eyes were twice their normal size. His mouth gaped open as he stared up at the mountain of a man. Drew thought he was going to cry.

"You've got it all wrong, mister," Drew blurted out before he thought. Reaching over he caught hold of a wrist that felt like iron. "The lady came up to him."

Why in the devil did I do that? Drew asked himself when the smiling brown giant slowly turned his head and leveled a patronizing glare down at him. Although Drew wasn't physically touched by the man, he could feel his life oozing away. He wanted to cry.

This man could kill me with one punch and I'm standing here arguing with him like a first-class fool!

"Are you amigos?" the Mexican asked wryly, batting his eyes impatiently.

"Yes," Drew said quickly, believing that would make a difference. All this time the girl stood sipping the champagne and really enjoying it — And no doubt the attention, too. A thought suddenly struck Drew. "Miss Zuniga, tell him how this happened." A prayer couldn't have sounded more imploring.

Bestowing a glowing smile on Drew, she nodded, the motion swaying the midnight-black hair.

"Sanyo," she purred, batting her long black lashes up at him, "he wanted to buy me a drink." Butter wouldn't have melted in her ruby-red mouth as she turned a dimpled and beguiling smile up at him. She had turned it around.

"But she—" Rick started to protest. Before he could say anything else, Sanyo grabbed a fistful of Rick's shirt, picked him up from the floor in one swift motion, and slammed him back against the bar. The impact knocked the air from Rick's lungs with a swoosh and doubled him forward. As if that wasn't bad enough, and to add insult to injury, Sanyo drew back his right ham-sized fist and smacked it squarely into Rick's face. Rick's head snapped back from the blow, which sent his hat tumbling behind the bar. Blood squirted from Rick's nose and mingled into his beard from a wide cut on his mouth.

Sanyo still had Rick's shirt gripped tightly in his hand and was shaking the bloody man like a limp rag doll. Drew knew that if Sanyo hit Rick that hard again it would kill him. There was only one thing for him to do.

Stepping well out of the burly man's reach, Drew pulled the Colt .45 from the holster and jabbed it against the hard-muscled side, pulling the hammer back at the same time.

"If you don't let him go," Drew said in a soft voice, "I'll blow a hole in you big enough to ride a horse through." There was no reason to speak loud because nobody was saying anything. All eyes were glued on the four people at the bar.

At first Sanyo was so engrossed in flailing the life out of Rick that he didn't pay any attention to Drew. But when Drew pressed the muzzle tighter against the big man's ribs, it got his attention.

Turning his head slowly, he looked at Drew and judged from the narrowed and deadly gleam in his eyes that Drew meant what he said. Opening his hand he let Rick drop in a bloody heap to the floor. Rick hit the floor with a thud and moan.

Keeping a wary eye on Sanyo, Drew eased over to Rick and helped him to his feet. The bartender handed Rick his hat and a wet towel, and he wiped away most of the blood. But his nose would never look the same. It was flattened against his face.

"Now, you big ox," Drew said in a level tone, "you're going to listen to what he has to say. If you try anything before he's through, I swear I'll shoot you where you stand." There was conviction in his voice.

Rick shook his head to clear away the buzzing, and blinked his eyes a couple of times.

"It's like I tried to tell you a while ago," he began hesitantly, his speech a little slurred. His upper lip didn't want to cooperate with the bottom. It looked like a shovel turned upside down. "She came up to us and asked me if I wanted to buy her a drink. I didn't know she belonged to you—or to *anybody*, for that matter. If I'd known that, I wouldn't have gotten this." Gently he touched his swelling nose and mouth, and moaned in pain. His eyes teared.

"Querida," Sanyo said lightly, gazing tenderly down at the demure woman smiling coyly up at him, "is what he says true?"

"Si, Sanyo," she confessed, fluttering her lashes up at him, "but I was so thirsty. The dance was so hot." With the movement of a stretching cat she eased away from the bar and slipped her arm through his.

"Annaletha," he chided softly, smiling down at her, "someday you will be the death of me." He bent down and, surprisingly for a man his size and bearing, tenderly kissed her red mouth.

"Amigos," he bellowed, turning toward Rick, who almost fainted at the movement, "my apologies. I just don't like for any men to touch my Annaletha. Let me buy you a drink." Slamming his fist down on the bar, Sanyo thundered for drinks to be served to everyone, on him.

Not wanting to anger the man again, Drew holstered the pistol and quickly tossed down a shot of good whiskey. Rick, thankful not to have any more pain and injury inflicted on him, drained the beer mug.

Sanyo looked over at Rick, threw back his massive head, and roared in laughter. But he sobered when he saw the angry frown on Rick's bearded and mangled face.

"Ah, amigo," he cajoled, reaching out and slapping Rick's shoulder, "you are still upset with me, eh?" He smiled, put his log-sized arm around Annaletha, and pulled her gently against him. "But can you blame me? When you have someone who looks like her, all clear thinking goes out of the head."

Painful memories pulled at Drew's heart and he blinked his eyes several times. He knew what Sanyo meant.

"Sanyo, that's the reason we're down here," Drew said coldly. "A man killed my wife at Fort Rather, Arizona, this week and we think he's here in Nogales. We don't mean any harm to anyone except the man we're looking for."

Someone of Sanyo's stature would no doubt have some power in town, and maybe he could help them.

A serious look replaced the grin on the wide brown face and his eyes narrowed thoughtfully.

"What does this son of a devil look like?" he questioned, a dark frown pulling his thick brows together. His brown eyes were almost black.

While Rick described Caleb Dayton to the big Mexican, Sanyo watched him intently. His eyes widened when Rick got to the part about Dayton riding a mule.

Whirling around from the bar, he faced the other customers and in rapid Spanish repeated what Drew and Rick had told him. But they either hadn't seen Dayton or weren't saying. They only shook their heads with blank and uncaring expressions on their faces.

"Is there a reward on this *hombre*?" Sanyo asked shrewdly, a twinkle gleaming in his eyes.

"No," Drew said shortly. "Rick and I are the only

ones who want him. I'll get him one way or the other."

"You wouldn't pay me to help you get him?" Sanyo bantered, cocking his head to one side, speculation raising an eyebrow.

"No," Drew snapped again. "All I want to know is if anyone here has seen this bearded old man. Ask them again."

Once more Sanyo asked the same question, and still no one said anything. Something told Drew that Dayton could be hiding under one of the tables and no one would tell.

"Let's try the other place," Drew said to Rick, and he started toward the door.

"Amigos," Sanyo called out. Drew stopped, one hand on the batwing, the other dropped to the pistol handle. "What should I do if I see this man who rides a mule?" Sarcasm edged his voice.

"Nothing," Drew said, turning around to face Sanyo. "He hasn't done anything to you. You have no reason to do anything to him. If you should *see* him before I do, I wish you'd try to find me. I'll be somewhere here in town. If something happens to him, you'll be sorry."

The two men stared at each other across the quiet saloon. Drew's blue eyes were cold and serious. Sanyo's brown eyes were twinkling.

Stunned patrons, even those who'd had more than enough to drink, turned their heads back and forth as each man spoke. No one had ever had enough nerve to go up against Sanyo before, and they didn't know what to think.

Throwing a last warning glance at Sanyo, Drew

stepped out into the street, Rick right behind him.

"What took you so dang long to draw down on that bear?" Rick asked, touching his mouth tenderly. "He nearly killed me!"

Drew wanted to laugh but didn't feel that now would be a good time. "It's simple," he replied, clearing his throat. "I wasn't the one his woman was hanging on to. He didn't have any quarrel with me."

"Well, I'm glad you finally stepped in when you did," Rick said flatly, his voice rising. A laugh burst from his throat. "I thought for a minute he was going to knock my teeth out. I won't be able to breathe through my nose for a year."

"Rick," Drew said patiently, shaking his head slowly and drawing his mouth into a thin line, "the man only hit you one time."

"Thank God for that," Rick replied, glaring at Drew. Their laughter filled the crowded street.

"If we don't find Dayton in this place," Rick asked as they neared the Placio de Plesur, "where do we look? My body can't take many more questions."

"I don't know," Drew said, shaking his head thoughtfully. "I really believe he's here in Nogales. But I also believed that he was heading back up north before, and was wrong. If he's not here, we'll just have to look somewhere else."

The exterior of Placio de Plesur was better than Try Your Luck and less than Noche de Oro. It was bigger and smaller, respectively. Drew felt a nervous sweat pop out on his face and neck as he reached out to open the batwings.

"Pssst." He heard the sound coming from the far side of the low wooden structure. Looking over his shoulder at Rick, Drew eased the pistol loose in the holster, walked past the door and around the corner of the building. He expected to find the boy waiting with some more information for money, but was more than surprised to see a girl maybe twelve years old huddled nervously against the wall. Her black eyes were large in fright and her brown arms were folded tightly across her chest.

"You have information for me, chiquita?" Drew asked, pushing the pistol back down into the holster. Some of the tenseness went out of her shoulders.

"Si, señor." She nodded rapidly, her long black hair swirling around her shoulders. "You are looking for older Americano riding a mule, no?"

"Yes," Drew answered gently, and, smiling, squatted down before her and placed his hands on her shoulders. "Don't be afraid. Nothing will happen to you."

Her brief, hesitant smile showed white teeth. He had no idea why he'd made such a statement. Had she see what Sanyo had done to Rick?

"The man you look for is hiding in the church." As soon as the rapid words were spoken, the girl clamped her mouth shut and gripped her brown hands behind her. Her small chest rose and fell in short breaths. She was scared half to death.

"The church!" Drew repeated, standing up, a frown of disbelief all over his face. "I would never have thought about that." Reaching into his pocket he took out two silver dollars and pressed them into the girl's hand. "Where is the church?" he asked, chewing on the inside of his mouth.

"At the far end of town," she answered, gesturing

to the east end of the street.

"Thanks, little one," Drew said absently, patting her head. "Run along and buy yourself some candy."

He and Rick waited until she'd disappeared down the street in the opposite direction before they went back out on the street.

"That old dog knows we're here," Rick observed hotly, adjusting the black hat on his head, "and he's playing it smart by holing up in the church. He thinks you won't come after him." Pausing, Rick looked at Drew for a second, his eyes narrow. "But you are, aren't you?"

Bringing his gaze slowly back to Rick, Drew nodded. Taking the Colt .45 from the holster, Drew spun the cylinder, replaced a spent cartridge, and replaced the pistol.

Walking in long strides back down the dusty street to the Try Your Luck, Drew and Rick got their horses, swung up in the saddle, and headed back the way they'd just come. A lot of Placio de Plesur customers were standing behind the batwings watching them ride past.

The white adobe church, with a bell tower, was far enough down the street to be away from any kind of noise. The saloon patrons and townspeople were either smart enough, or not interested enough, and didn't follow them to see what would happen when they caught up with Dayton.

Drew and Rick tied their horses to the hitch rail in front of the church, went up the three low stone steps, and pushed open the heavy wooden door.

The interior of the church was cool and dim. Candles flickered by the door, at the confessionals, and up around the altar. Various statues and crucifixes hung on the walls or were on stands around the church. The surroundings were so peaceful that for a split second Drew forgot why there were there. This was a place for prayer, peace, and quiet. Not for carrying out an act of revenge and hatred.

He was jerked back to full alertness when he heard the soft slapping of sandals on the stone floor. A middle-aged gray-haired priest came shuffling toward them, his long black robe just missing the top of his feet. His hands were folded and hidden in the big sleeves of the robe. A gold cross and beads swung from a belt around his pudgy waist, with the motion of his plump body. The priest's hazel eyes didn't miss anything, and he knew the two Americans standing there with their guns tied down low didn't want to make any confessions. His eyes widened a little when he looked at Rick's swollen face.

"Welcome to the Holy Angels Church, my sons," he said in a soft, solicitous voice, bowing his head just a little. "I am Father Miguel Acquello. How may I help you?"

Something in the way the priest looked at them told Drew that he knew exactly why there were there. Drew also knew he'd have a hard time getting information out of him.

"We're looking for Caleb Dayton," Drew said simply, pushing his hat back. "He's old, tall, and has a red beard. He's supposed to be riding a mule."

All kinds of decisions were made in the priest's mind in the few seconds it took Drew to tell him why they were at at the church. His eyes shifted from Drew back to Rick and back to Drew again. The little priest apparently wasn't used to telling lies, and had to construct something plausible in his mind.

"I was told he was hiding here," Drew prompted, looking him straight in the eye. "Is he here?"

More time passed before Acquello decided to answer with the truth.

"Si," he replied, nodding twice, "he is here. But I cannot say he is hiding. Why are you looking for him? Is he a friend of yours?" The expression in his eyes told Drew he knew what the answer would be.

"Not hardly," Drew answered dryly, shaking his head rapidly. He was about to lose his patience and knew he was in the wrong place to do it. "He killed my wife and daughter three days ago at Fort Rather, Arizona."

Drew was angered when the priest quickly crossed himself and whispered a quick prayer. Was he praying for Melissa and Little Moon? Or Dayton? Or for him?

"Tell him to come out," Rick snapped, resting his hand on the pistol handle. He looked around the church for the obvious hiding places. One confessional was on either side of the narrow aisle, and a door up at the front right-hand side which probably led to the priest's office were the only likely places anyone could hide. When the priest hesitated, Rick started forward. But Acquello held up his hand and stopped him.

"You cannot do that," he protested sternly, shaking his head slowly. "Señor Dayton has the protection of the Church, just as you would in a similar situation. I must ask you to leave, if you are here only to cause trouble."

Knowing the priest was right, Drew admitted they had no choice. Dayton could stay in the church from now until the saints came and there was nothing he could do about it. The priest would feed Dayton and he'd have a place to sleep. At the moment, Drew's hands were tied.

"Let's go, Rick," he said loudly and started down the aisle. Rick looked at him as if he couldn't believe what he was hearing.

"You're not going to just walk away, are you?" Rick asked, confusion pulling a frown between his brows.

"Yeah," Drew replied loudly again. "Dayton's got us bested. We'll have to try some other way." Taking some coins from his pocket, he dropped them into the poorbox. Rick did the same.

Closing the door behind them as they stepped out into the waning sunlight, Drew pushed his hat back on his head and grinned slyly at Rick.

"Why in the Sam Hill were you yelling so dang loud?" Rick asked as they mounted and headed east. Drew couldn't tell if the frown on Rick's face was from irritation or puzzlement. "You nearly busted my eardrums."

"I wanted Dayton to hear me," Drew answered, a malicious smile spreading across his face. "I wanted him to believe that we're giving up."

Rick shook his head disdainfully. He knew Drew's idea wasn't going to work.

"He's not stupid, Drew," Rick argued slowly, cocking an eyebrow. "You know he was watching us. I'll bet you anything he was hiding in one of those little rooms where you tell all your sins to the priest."

Drew threw back his head and roared in hearty laughter.

"Have you ever told anybody all the bad things you've done?" he asked, clearing his throat.

"Naw," Rick replied, shaking his head and pulling his mouth to one side. "I've never considered the things I've done interesting enough, or anybody's business, to tell them. Have you?"

Drew was thoughtful for a minute, then somberly shook his head. "No," he finally answered. "I've never felt the need to tell a man what sins I've done. God already knows it anyway. But I guess the worst things I've done was kill Yankee soldiers and then the Dayton brothers. All of that could come under the heading of duty, I guess. This thing with Caleb Dayton is really revenge for killing Melissa and Little Moon. Is revenge a sin?"

"Don't start me to lying," Rick said, shrugging his shoulders and squinting his eyes against the glare of the setting sun on the white rocks. "Other than the war, I've only killed one man, and that was in self-defense in a barroom brawl."

They had ridden well past the outskirts of town and up into the hills, but still had a good view of the church. Dismounting, they tied the horses to a scrub bush, then sat down under an outcropping of rock to watch and wait for Dayton to leave the church. Until he did that, there was nothing else for them to do.

Chapter IV

Minutes ran into hours and the shadows lengthened toward the east. The red sun faded into an orange ball and was slipping noticeably faster down in the pale blue sky behind the mountains. Purple shadows, then velvet darkness, settled over the land. Drew and Rick watched the church like vultures would a wounded animal just waiting for the right time to move in. From their two vantage points they could see three sides of the church, and if anyone left the building they would be able to see them if they rode in the other direction.

"Do you think Dayton will spend the night at the church?" Rick asked, getting up from the rock and rubbing his backside.

"I don't know," Drew replied, standing up and kicking his legs to get the kinks out. "If he does, there isn't anything we can do about it." In the vanishing light the men stared at each other, the same thought flashing in their mind.

"Why don't we take a ride back to the church and see if Dayton's still there?" Drew said shrewdly. "I don't like the gut feeling I'm getting." Something told him that Dayton had given them the slip again.

Rick had been looking toward the church but jerked around to face Drew, a frown on his face. Tightening the cinches on the horses, they mounted and headed back at a fast gallop the way they'd ridden at least two hours ago.

"What kind of gut feeling are you getting?" Rick asked, squinting his blue eyes slyly.

"Well," Drew said, drawing his mouth to one side in a sucking sound, "if he was slick enough to come up on our camp last night, then get away without leaving much of a trail, and then be mean enough to hide in a church, he'll do anything. It wouldn't surprise me if he's already left Nogales."

"Oh, I don't think he's left Nogales," Rick drew out slowly as they galloped along. "You know what he said about getting you." When Drew nodded, Rick went on: "He'd hang around to see if he could make a fool out of us again."

Anger rushed over Drew and he gritted his teeth so hard that his jaw ached. Rick had just put words to what he couldn't or wouldn't admit to himself about his feelings when Dayton had found them last night. He didn't mind having jokes played on him, but he didn't like being made a fool of—especially twice by the same person.

By the time they had ridden down from the hills and pulled the horses to a stop in front of the church, the moon was peeping over the horizon and throwing silver shadows on everything.

They'd seen a light in a small window at the back of the church, and reasoned that the priest either had an office back there or that it was where he slept. After Drew knocked on the door, it took a little while for the priest to get there.

Apparently, the priest did not recognize Drew and Rick at first, and only saw two men standing there.

"How can I help you, my sons?" he asked in the same solicitous voice as before. For some reason the sugary tone rubbed Drew the wrong way and his stomach tightened. He'd probably ask the devil the same thing!

"We were here earlier," Drew said without any preliminaries or extending title courtesy. "We're still looking for Caleb Dayton. He's not here, is he?"

The priest folded his hands in front of him, unable to hide a disgusted look as he finally recognized Drew. Taking a deep breath he dropped his head, slowly raised it, looked Drew straight in the eye, and finally shook his head.

"No," he said curtly, expelling the breath. "He left about two hours ago." There was no remorse or guilt on the priest's face or in his voice. He was only stating a fact when he answered the question. It didn't seem to bother him either when Drew's face turned a brilliant red and his blue eyes snapped in anger.

"Why didn't you stop him?" Drew demanded in a low voice, glaring down at the priest. As soon as the question was out he knew it was stupid.

"Señor, I couldn't have stopped him even if I had wanted to," Acquello replied passively. "He had done nothing against the Church. He said he need a safe place to stay for a while. The Church is a place of safety and peace for everyone. I could not turn him away no more than I could you and your friend if you needed help."

Drew was so angry he knew he'd explode if he stayed much longer. He wanted to reach out, grab this pious priest by the robe, and shake him until his beads rattled. The look must have told Acquello what was in Drew's mind, because his face turned white and he stepped back, well out of Drew's reach.

"Do you still intend to kill this man?" Acquello

asked, a sad expression in his hazel eyes. His fear had been replaced by his faith, even though the priest knew from Drew's look that it took a lot of will power for Drew not to do bodily harm to him.

"Yes, I still intend to kill him," Drew answered snidely, a snarl curling his lips back. Blue ice couldn't have been any colder than Drew's eyes.

"I will say a prayer for both of you," Acquello said softly, crossing himself rapidly and shaking his head.

"You'd better say two prayers for Dayton," Drew suggested, breathing hard. "Did he say where he was going?" His eyes were steady and his voice level.

"All I can tell you," the priest said, folding his hands inside the sleeves, "is he said it was time to go back to hunting. He said it would be easier now. Before you ask," he hurried on when he saw Drew was about to interrupt, "I did not ask what he was hunting."

"Come on, Drew," Rick said in disgust, reaching out and catching Drew's arm, "let's go. We've wasted enough of the priest's time." This time they didn't put any money in the poorbox.

Without saying anything else the two men left the church, got back on their horses, and rode toward town. Darkness made the way seem a lot longer.

"What do you think?" Drew asked, his anger subsiding a little.

"I don't know what to think about this old man," Rick answered. There was some admiration in Rick's voice, and it both surprised and aggravated Drew. But when he thought about it for a second, he did agree with Rick. Caleb Dayton was a crafty man, and it would take a lot of luck for Drew and Rick to outsmart him.

Hunger pains began gnawing at Drew's stomach and he realized that they hadn't eaten since early that morning.

"What do you say about us getting some food?" he suggested, glancing at Rick.

"I thought you'd never ask," Rick replied, rubbing his stomach. "Do you think there's a place in this so-called town that has food good enough to eat? My stomach can't stand beans and bread tonight. I need some meat." They laughed at the jest but they both knew they were entitled to a good meal.

"Well, neither of the saloons had food," Drew pointed out, "and I don't think you'd want to go back to Placio de Plesur anyway, unless you want to visit with Lady Lashes and that bear again."

"Hunger has made you crazy," Rick said, squinting and shaking his head. They both laughed again.

They didn't attract as much attention this time, riding down the street as they had before in the daylight. They weren't in such a hurry now and rode slower, paying more attention to the buildings. They were surprised to see a small cafe on the west side of Noche de Oro.

Dismounting in a rush they weren't aware of, they tied the horses to the wooden rack and almost ran into the cafe. A spicy mixture of aromas made their mouths water and they wasted no time getting a table in the corner.

A tall thin black-haired Mexican wearing a food-stained white shirt and pants started their way slowly, then hurried when they beckoned to him.

"We want a lot of whatever you have," Drew said,

pushing his hat back and patting his stomach. "But not too hot."

"I don't care how hot it is," Rick said, rubbing his hands together. "We can wash it down with beer. I'm so hungry I could eat a table. But no beans."

The waiter coughed and Drew looked up at him. A sly grin was twinkling in his black eyes and pulling his mouth into a thin line. Drew had a sneaking suspicion what the man had in mind, and he felt sorry for Rick for what was about to happen to him.

"Could you just hurry?" Drew said, wanting to laugh.

Nodding, the waiter turned, went to the kitchen, and soon returned with two plates piled high with beans, tamales, potatoes, tortillas, chili, a hunk of onion, and green peppers. Drew glanced at both plates. To him they both looked the same. Drew and Rick waited until the waiter had returned with two mugs of beer before starting to eat.

Stepping back out of Rick's sight, the waiter leaned against the wall and crossed his arms over his chest, amused expectation on his brown face.

Drew and Rick took long swigs of beer and washed down long hours and miles of dust.

"That does taste good," Rick said, smacking his lips. Picking up the fork, he cut off a piece of tamale, dipped it in the chili, put it into his mouth, and began chewing.

Suddenly he stopped, his features frozen. His face turned red, almost purple, and his blue eyes began watering. Swallowing with effort he jumped up, turning over the chair. He gritted his teeth until a knot popped up in his jaw. Jerking up the mug he sloshed the beer over the side and took a long pull. Then he expelled a long breath.

"What's wrong, Rick?" Drew asked, looking up at him and blinking his eyes innocently. "Is it hot enough for you?"

"God a'mighty!" Rick choked out, gasping for breath, tears rolling from his eyes and down into his beard. "I've never had anything so hot in all my life."

"I thought you didn't care how hot the food was," Drew reminded, cocking an eyebrow and pursing his lips.

"Well," Rick said, coughing and clearing his throat, "there's hot food, and then there's food that's just this side of Hades." With the back of his hands he wiped the tears from his eyes. Picking up the chair he plopped down on it, took and exhaled a deep breath again.

Drew heard someone clap his hands together, and looked up to see what was going on. The waiter was doubled over in hysterical laughter. Straightening up, he came over the table and patted Rick on the shoulder.

"Do not be angry with me, señor," he said, blinking his black eyes. "I hope the food did not burn your mouth too much. I could not resist the trick."

In mock anger Rick glared up at him and shook his head.

"How could it have burned too much?" Drew put in, trying not to laugh again. "He didn't have it in his mouth long enough." In spite of his efforts he burst out laughing again.

"Let me have your plate," the waiter requested, reaching down for it, "and I will get you something better."

"Gladly," Rick said, handing him the hardly touched plate. "Was he trying to kill me?" he asked glibly, squinting his eyes dubiously when the waiter disappeared.

"No," Drew answered slowly, smiling snidely at him. "He was only trying to get you to eat your words." Again he burst out laughing, and slapped his hands down on the table.

The waiter returned soon with another filled plate. Rick test it gingerly, nodded his head, and began eating ravenously.

Their plates were soon empty, and when Drew held up his hand to summon the waiter for another mug of beer he asked him if he'd seen Dayton. He was angered and surprised when the waiter nodded.

"Si, señor. About two hours ago he came in," he answered, a frown between his black eyes. "He ate a plateful just like the first one I brought you." He inclined his head toward Rick.

Real anger rushed over Drew! While they were waiting and watching the church in the dust and heat, Dayton had been enjoying himself with a good meal and beer.

"Did he say anything to you?" Drew asked, feeling silly asking the same question again. If their luck didn't change soon, they'd be old and gray before finding this sneaky old man.

"Only that he'd played a trick on fools again," the waiter answered, still frowning and narrowing his eyes. For a reason that puzzled Drew, the waiter shifted his gaze quickly from Drew to Rick, then back to Drew again. "Are you the two fools he played the trick on?"

Drew felt like he'd been hit in the face with a wet rag. Not only had Dayton outsmarted them again, he was bragging about it and calling them names!

"Well," Drew snapped, nodding, draining the mug, and slamming it down on the table, "if he said all of that, did he say where he was going when he left here?"

The waiter thought for a second, a perplexed expression narrowing his eyes even more.

"Only that there was some hunting he had to do," he replied, folding his hands behind his back. It was then that it dawned on Drew the difference between this tall dark-skinned man and the other Mexicans he'd come in contact with lately: he lacked a subservient attitude. He'd even gone out of his way to play a joke on Rick without thinking of the consequence, and he wasn't afraid to give them information.

"He didn't say any more than that about where he was going?" Drew insisted, a tone in his voice that brought a strange look to the waiter's face.

"No," he answered, shaking his head slowly. "May I ask you a question?"

"Sure, why not," Drew answered, shrugging his shoulders, pushing back his hat.

"Why are you so interested in this old man?" Something told him that things weren't right here. "If you knew he was in town earlier, why didn't you find him?"

The question was simple. Only the answer was complicated.

"We knew he was in town," Rick said, wrinkling his forehead. "In fact, we were in the same building with him. The only problem, he was hiding in the church."

"Oh, I see," the waiter drew out, nodding slowly. "Are you lawmen?"

"No," Drew answered, shaking his head disdainfully. "Even if we were, it wouldn't matter or help down here. I might as well tell you. This old man, Caleb Dayton, killed my wife and daughter. I want him! He's going to pay for what he did."

The waiter's black eyes widened in astonishment and his mouth dropped open. "Oh, señor, I am sorry," he said softly, slowly shaking his head sorrowfully. "He only said he had some hunting to do. He finished eating, then left."

The waiter walked off when someone else called him. Drew and Rick finished eating, put some money down on the table, and stepped out into the warm night air.

"Wonder what he meant by some hunting?" Drew questioned, standing by the horse, the reins in one hand, the other hand on the back of the saddle.

"Does he mean us or buffalo?" Rick asked, swinging up on Money Man.

"Oh, he doesn't mean us," Drew answered pointedly, setting himself down on the saddle. "He knows exactly where we are. Maybe he meant he's going up to Montana where there are a lot of buffalo, after he gets through playing with us and finishes us off." But, Drew didn't believe what he'd just said.

They rode to the edge of town and stopped when Drew pulled his horse to an abrupt halt.

"I know Dayton is watching every move we make," Drew said, expelling a deep breath. "We'd be sitting ducks if we camped out tonight. Why don't we get a room at the hotel?"

Drew couldn't believe how scared he was. Cold chills ran up and down his back, and he felt sick to his stomach. He hadn't been this scared even when all three Dayton brothers had been after him.

"Sounds good to me," Rick agreed. "I feel like Dayton could reach out and scratch my back."

The levity in Rick's voice brought nervous laughter from Drew.

Turning the horses around, they rode back into town and stopped in front of a two-story hotel. The low-ceilinged lobby was stifling hot when they went in carrying bedrolls, saddlebags, and rifles.

Surprisingly, a white man pushed a thick register across the rough desk. His glance told him the two men were only a couple of saddle tramps passing through town.

"Is the front room empty?" Drew asked, dipping the quill pen into the small bottle of black ink and signing for them. A thought was building in the back of his mind.

"Sure" was the short sullen answer. He shoved the key toward Drew and held out his hand. Reaching into his pocket Drew pulled out some of the reward money on Dayton and handed it to the man. It gave him a good feeling to know that in a roundabout way Dayton was paying for his room. He picked up his bedroll, saddlebag, and key, then he and Rick started up the stairs.

"Would you mind telling me why in the heck you wanted a front room?" Rick asked, disbelief in his voice as they walked down the carpeted hall. In the dim light of an oil lamp hanging on the wall, Drew saw a frown on Rick's bearded face.

"It should be obvious," Drew replied, putting the key in the lock and opening the door. "If somebody should try to get in, we could hear them better coming through a window than down the hall."

Rick thought a minute, pondering the logic of Drew's idea, then nodded in agreement.

They didn't light the oil lamp on the wall. The moonlight was enough for them to see their way around the sparsely furnished room. Rick braced a straight-backed chair under the doorknob.

Undressing down to their underwear they stretched out on the bed that was a far cry from the ground they'd slept on last night. Drew took the side by the window, pulled the other straight-backed chair close to the side of the bed, and dropped his gun belt over it, the pistol handle only inches from his hand. Rick laid his heavy gun on the small table by the bed, within easy reach.

Whether it was from total mental and physical exhaustion, they would later wonder, but they heard no sounds at all during the entire night. As was Drew's habit he awoke when the first gray streaks of dawn were dividing the earth from the sky.

Reaching over, Drew shook Rick awake, then pulled on his pants and boots. Standing up he put his shirt on, and stretched as he walked over to the window. He didn't believe what he saw and it took a little while for it to sink in. Then it hit him like a bolt of lightning. His horse was gone! Only Money Man, Rick's gelding, was still tied to the hitch rail in front of the hotel. In their haste for a good night's sleep they'd forgotten to put the horses in the livery. That probably wouldn't have made any difference anyway.

"Damn," Drew shouted, gritting his teeth. Anger and disbelief edged his voice. Strapping the gun around his waist he started for the door, jerking up his bedroll, saddlebags, and rifle on the way.

"What's wrong?" Rick asked, pulling his clothes on. His speech was still sleep-slurred, and his swollen lip didn't help much, either.

"My horse is gone!" Drew snapped, glaring at Rick and shaking his head.

"What do you mean?" Rick asked, frowning. "Your horse or both?"

"Just mine," Drew shouted tightly, disgust raw in his voice and eyes.

Charging down the stairs, across the lobby, and out on the sidewalk, Drew stopped short in his tracks. Rick was right on his heels. A white piece of paper, tied to the saddle horn, was flapping in the gentle morning breeze.

Something told Drew the note was from Caleb Dayton and was meant for him. Running over to Money Man, he dropped the saddlebags and bedroll on the ground and jerked the paper off. In crude printing the words leaped out at him:

I lost thre thangs. Yev jest lost to. Wun mor ta go.

Drew stared at the black-penciled letters. They ran together in one long blurred line. Cold then hot rage surged through Drew, and he'd never wanted to kill anyone as much in his life as he did Caleb Dayton just then.

"When I get my hands on that scum," Drew threatened between clenched teeth, his hands gripped into fists at his side, "I swear there won't be enough left of him for an ant to chew on! Let's find a livery. I've got to get a horse!"

They started down the street, Rick leading his horse, toward a building that appeared to be a stable or small livery. They'd gone about halfway when a lazy familiar voice stopped them.

"Heeey, amigos." Drew stopped. Scared to. Scared not to. Anything could happen with the man who was speaking so softly behind them. Turning slowly, his hand on the handle of the Colt .45, Drew looked Sanyo squarely in the eye. The big Mexican stood in front of the Placio de Plesur leaning against the porch support. He was dressed the same as yesterday. A dazzling white shirt was unbuttoned all the way down, the ends tucked inside black pants. He held a half-full bottle in one hand, a shot glass in the other.

"Good morning, Sanyo," Drew greeted caustically, arching an eyebrow. "How are you this fine morning? Did you beat up anyone else last night? Did you sleep well?" Drew's sarcasm did him good.

Sanyo threw back his massive black head and his hearty laughter filled the otherwise-empty street.

"Oh, no, señors," he replied slowly, wrinkling his forehead and smiling broadly. "That was truly a mistake." Looking at Rick he made a low bow and straightened up. "I see you have only one horse. What happened to the other one?"

Drew didn't like wasting time, but on the other hand he didn't want to rile Sanyo, either. The big man had a short fuse and it wouldn't take much to set him off.

Might as well tell him the truth and get it over with, Drew decided, walking back toward him and stopping at what he hoped was a safe distance.

"The old man we're looking for was hiding in the church," he began, dropping the saddlebags to the ground. "We couldn't touch him because he was protected by the Church and a priest. He told the priest he was leaving town and we believed him. But the old dog lied. He hid somewhere here in town and took my horse after we went to bed last night."

Drew felt silly standing there in the dusty street of Nogales, Mexico, with the sun already beginning to warm things, telling this tale of woe to a man who couldn't possibly care less.

"Ah, señor," Sanyo said sadly, pouring more of whatever it was he was drinking into a glass. "A man without a horse in this country might as well be dead. You cannot find this man if you are walking, no?" A slick smile played on his slightly slack mouth.

Drew got the feeling from the sly gleam in Sanyo's black eyes that some kind of idea was taking root there.

"You're right," Drew agreed, nodding slowly, watching Sanyo intently, a knot tightening in his stomach. What was Sanyo up to?

"I'll tell you what," Sanyo said, coming off the sidewalk. "I still feel bad about yesterday. I want to make it right with you. Come."

Motioning with a massive arm, Sanyo walked past Drew, up to Rick, slapped him lightly on the shoulder, then continued on down the street in the direction Drew and Rick had been going when he'd stopped them. They had no choice but to follow him. The man was still walking straight, but a little something in his step told Drew that Sanyo was well on his way to getting drunk.

Drew was dumbfounded when Sanyo stopped at the livery, opened the door, and went in. Rick waited outside while Drew went in behind Sanyo. Drew was even more shocked when the man who'd handled Rick like a rag last night gently put a gray and black blanket on the broad, smooth back of a stallion as white as his shirt. Removing a silver-covered saddle from a rack, Sanyo put it over the blanket, tightened the cinch, untied the reins, and led the horse over to Drew.

"I know you would help me if you had to," Sanyo said, the wide smile showing strong white teeth. "So, Nino Blanca is yours."

Sanyo looked like a little boy offering someone his last bite of candy. Drew couldn't believe this. He wouldn't give anybody a horse that looked like the one standing so proudly before him. Sanyo couldn't be serious. That horse, not to mention the saddle, was worth a lot of money. Then it dawned on Drew. Sanyo was drunk. He had to be. No man in his right mind—if he was sober—would do such a stupid thing.

"Sanyo," Drew began, grinning slightly and shaking his head, "I can't take that horse. Or that saddle. They're too valuable. What would you ride?"

Turning his head slowly, Sanyo squinted his eyes into narrow slits. "Do not worry, señor," he said, smiling. "I will not walk." Walking further back into the livery he was gone only a short while, then returned leading a golden palomino with a cream-colored mane and tail. Pride and satisfaction gleamed in Sanyo's dark eyes. Arching his brows, Sanyo inclined his head.

"Sanyo, I'll take the horse," Drew relented, shrugging his shoulders, "only because I have to. But I can't take that saddle. It's too valuable. I'll just take that old one there on the railing. When I find Dayton, I'll get my own horse and saddle back and return yours."

The saddle Drew meant was an old one of cracked brown leather that had seen a lot of use many years ago.

"As you wish," Sanyo relented, spreading his hands and shrugging his wide shoulders. "Is there anything more I can do for you?"

"No," Drew answered, taking off the ornate saddle and replacing it with the old one. "I don't know why you're doing this, Sanyo, but I really do appreciate it. Thanks a lot."

Drew swung up on the white horse, which skittered a little at the unfamiliar man, and sat on the rough leather.

"I wanted to prove to you that I am not as bad as you doubtless think I am," Sanyo answered pensively. "If you find your horse and come back this way, you can bring Nino Blanco. If not, that is all right." Sanyo reached up his huge hand. Without any hesitation Drew reached down and shook hands with the man who could have put him out of this world with just one punch from that same hand.

Drew breathed a long sigh of relief when he rode out of the livery and up beside Rick, whose eyes almost popped out of their sockets when he saw what Drew was riding.

"I kind of thought he was going to offer you a

horse," he said, shaking his head in dismay. "But I thought it would be some old nag. Not something that Montezuma would ride! Do you want to trade?" He arched his brows.

For a brief moment Drew forgot about Caleb Dayton, if that was possible, and allowed himself a good feeling and laugh.

"Are you crazy?" he answered, reaching over and taking his saddlebags and bedroll from Rick and tying them behind him. "If this was yours, would you trade?"

Rick shook his head rapidly. Drew kneed the horse in the side and they started riding out of town. The horse had a smooth and easy gait. Out of pure curiosity, Drew turned around in the saddle. Somehow he wasn't too surprised to see Sanyo standing out in the middle of the street looking their way. He waved, and Drew returned the gesture.

"Which way do we go?" Rick asked, looking a little enviously at the white horse that was almost prancing along.

"Since we really don't know which way Dayton went," Drew answered, pushing his hat back, "why don't we do the same thing as before and ride a circle around Nogales." When Rick nodded, Drew went on, "This time it will be easier to find a track. My horse has a half-moon crack on the right back shoe."

Time passed and the sun climbed higher in the sky, throwing its hot rays down on the men and horses. All the while they rode, they had the feeling they were being watched.

Drew didn't think it was by Dayton, though. He was probably back in Arizona by now and laughing his head off at them. A bell in the back of his head told him their watchers were either Yaqui Indians or bandits. Either would kill at the drop of a hat for the white horse. Maybe Sanyo hadn't done him such a big favor after all. Had Sanyo set them up? Or had he planned something for Drew and Rick? He was drunk. When he sobered up and found the white horse gone, would he come after them for horse stealing?

I can't worry about that now, Drew told himself. I've got more important things on my mind.

They'd ridden about an hour and a half and were going northeast when Rick pulled back on the reins and jerked Money Man sharply to the right.

"Drew, come here," he called out loudly. Drew, about two hundred yards away, heard the urgency in Rick's voice and kneed Nino Blanco in the side. In no time the long white legs had covered the distance and Drew was looking down at a half-moon crack in the loose sand where Rick was pointing.

Dismounting in the shade of a twenty-foot cactus, Drew squatted down for a closer look at the two sets of hoofprints. There were no footprints, and Drew frowned. Suddenly a thought struck him. Was Dayton riding his horse? Hot anger shot over him.

Jumping up, he swung back into the saddle and started off in the same direction without saying anything to Rick.

Kicking Money Man in the side, Rick soon caught up with Drew, and he could tell from the dark frown on Drew's face that he was in a world of his own thoughts.

"What's wrong?" Rick called out. He was beginning to believe that he'd made a big mistake by coming along on this vengeance ride with Drew. All that they'd accomplished so far was spending two nights—one outside, the other in a hotel—away from the fort, himself almost getting beaten to death by a man who'd make two of him, and Drew getting a beautiful horse to replace the one stolen by an old man they were looking for. That didn't add up to very much and certainly didn't balance in the plus or minus columns. Everything was against them so far.

Drew seemed to be oblivious to hunger, but the rumbling noise in Rick's stomach made him realize that they hadn't eaten anything since last night.

"If what I'm thinking is true," Drew answered, turning his head to look at Rick, "Dayton is riding my horse. That's another reason I want to kill him! Nobody rides my horse!" Staring down at the saddle horn for a second, he jerked his head up and looked at Rick again. "Do you think I'm crazy for doing this?"

"No," Rick answered quickly, shaking his head, remembering the dressing-down he'd gotten before, when Drew had asked him the same question and he'd disagreed. "It's something you've got to do. I'd do the same thing." Rick was beginning to worry about Drew.

A tightness went out of Drew's shoulders and he relaxed a little. He shook his head sharply as if clearing his thoughts.

"Are you hungry?" he asked, a frown between his brows. "We haven't eaten in a long time, you know. What were you thinking?"

"About eating," Rick replied quickly again, and he looked curiously at Drew. His cousin was under a lot of strain, and something told him that it wouldn't take much for Drew to go off the deep end.

They rode on until several scrub trees offered a little

shade, and they dismounted. Dayton had been kind enough to leave the grub sack that was tied to Rick's horse. Drew opened a can of beans while Rick cut a piece of stale bread in half and took some jerky from a smaller sack.

Stretching out on the ground, they were quiet while they ate the dry bread, washing it down with swallows of tepid water.

"He's probably watching in those mountains right now," Drew said, sitting up and looking around at the towering granite summits above them. "All we can do is stay on this northeast trail and see what happens."

They sand-cleaned the plates and knives and put them back into the grub sack. The empty bean can was lying on the ground where Drew had dropped it, and was now completely covered with red ants. Ants bigger than Drew had ever seen. He let his mind wander and could see Caleb Dayton being eaten alive by those same ants. He shivered at the morbid thought.

"That would be a horrible way to go, wouldn't it?" Rick's voice snapped him back to the present. Drew was surprised at being caught with such open thoughts.

"How did you know what I was thinking?" Drew asked, squinting his eyes.

"It was written all over your face," Rick replied contritely, watching him intently. "What exactly are you going to do to Dayton?" Rick asked, tying the grub sack on the back of the saddle.

"I'm not sure," Drew said, shaking his head and swinging up into the saddle. "I've had so many ideas that my brain is tired. The only thing I'm sure of is that Caleb Dayton will die one way or the other when I find him."

They started the slow climb up the mountains. Rocks,

dislodged by the horses' feet, rolled down the way they'd just come. No kind of vegetation was visible as they went higher and higher. Behind every rock was an ideal place for an ambush, and Drew began breathing hard. He knew something was going to happen in a little while.

After a half hour of riding they came out on a plateau that gave them a view of the valley to the south, where they'd just been, and of open desert to the northeast. Suddenly a tiny moving speck in the north caught Drew's eye.

"Do you have any binoculars?" he asked Rick, his heart slamming against his ribs. In his haste to leave Fort Rather he'd forgotten to pack his.

"No binoculars," Rick answered, reaching back into his saddlebag, "but I've got a spyglass."

Drew thought it took forever for Rick to hand over the long collapsible tube and for him to get it pulled out. When he did, and put it up to his eye, he wasn't disappointed to see a man in a floppy-brimmed black hat riding his horse and leading a mule!

"There he is," Drew said in a low voice, knowing that every little sound carried easily in this kind of country. Pitching the glass back to Rick, Drew jerked the rifle from the worn scabbard and up to his shoulder. His finger was squeezing down on the trigger, and he caught himself just in time.

He didn't want to kill Dayton like this! He wanted him alive, so he'd know for sure who was doing it and why.

Shoving the rifle back down into the scabbard he kicked the white horse in the side. Apparently the horse wasn't used to such harsh treatment. Shaking his head frantically he snorted, pawed the ground, then almost threw Drew off when he reared up. Leaning forward

Drew tightened his knees to hang on.

Nino Blanco came back down, slamming his shod hoofs hard into the dry, packed ground. Then he took off running at a pace that almost dislodged Drew from the saddle. Regaining his balance he let the horse run. Hearing Money Man's pounding hoofs behind him, Drew knew Rick's horse had about as much power as the white stallion under him.

The trail that Dayton was leaving wasn't straight, by any means. It twisted and turned in and out of the rocks. But at the speed the horses were able to go, and knowing that after a while the mule would slow the old man down, Drew was confident that he'd have Dayton in only a matter of minutes! Then his mission would be over and Melissa and Little Moon could rest in peace.

Drew wasn't worried when they rode out of a draw and Dayton wasn't to be seen. Dayton was far enough ahead of them to disappear for a while, but Drew was sure they'd spot him soon.

But when they came out of the second draw and topped a rise, the moving figures of Dayton, the horse, and mule weren't what Drew and Rick saw. Drew's heart stopped in his chest and his blood ran cold.

If he hadn't known for certain that he was awake, Drew would have sworn he was having a nightmare.

Flanking both sides of the rise were six of the meanest-looking Indians Drew had ever seen. The two in front had Winchesters aimed down at them. Drew would later wonder where they'd gotten them. The other four had bows and quivers full of arrows.

These Indians didn't resemble Half Moon's people in any way.

The shoulder-length brown hair had an orangy tinge

to it. They were dressed similarly in light cotton shirts and pants. All wore calf-high moccasin boots and white straw hats. Hate-filled pale brown eyes watched them steadily.

"Oh, my God," Rick moaned softly. He closed his eyes and expelled a deep breath. "What do we do? Try and make a run for it?"

"We'd be crazy to run," Drew replied solemnly. "He'd shoot us in a breath." The cold look in the Indian's brown eyes told Drew he was right. "I've had the feeling all morning that we were being watched. I thought it was Dayton. But it was them."

At the sound of Drew's and Rick's voices the Indians exchanged words in a guttural sound that really sent shivers up and down Drew's back.

"What do they want?" Rick asked, easing Money Man over closer to him.

"One of two things," Drew replied slowly, watching the Indians steadily. "Us or the horses."

Chapter V

Without any warning, the one Drew thought of as the leader leaned over, holding the Winchester by the barrel like a bat, and knocked him out of the saddle, then aimed the rifle at him almost daring him to try anything. Rage narrowed the pale brown eyes. Thin lips were drawn down against his teeth in an animal-like snarl.

Following the leader's example, the other brave holding a Winchester knocked Rick from his horse but grinned menacingly down at him.

A burning sensation in his arm pulled Drew's eyes from the Yaqui's angry brown face. Blood was oozing from a cut on his shoulder where he'd hit a jagged piece of rock. Drew started to get up, but the leader lashed out with his moccasined foot and kicked him viciously in the face. Drew felt and heard his nose break, and tasted blood as it ran into his mouth. Black spots danced before his eyes.

"You slimy heathen," Rick growled, moving his hand slowly toward his pistol. But the grinning Yaqui was watching him closely, as if waiting for him to try such a thing. Using the rifle butt he clouted Rick across the left jaw.

The leader said something indistinguishable to one of the men behind him. In a series of easy movements, the Indian slid from his horse, took two leather thongs from his belt, and tied Drew's and Rick's hands behind them. In a swift motion he pulled them to their feet with a hard yank and shoved them forward. The pain from the cut brought a groan from Drew, and the Indian jerked him again, a malicious snarl curling his lips back. Then he picked up their rifles and pistols.

"Where do you suppose they're taking us?" Rick asked in a whisper, walking as close to Drew as possible so his voice wouldn't be as easily heard by the Yaquis.

"To their camp, I guess," Drew whispered back, his mouth beginning to swell from the kick. Now he knew how Rick had felt when Sanyo smashed his mouth yesterday. Had it only been yesterday? It seemed like such a long time ago.

Turning west, the leader started out at a pace just under a run. It was difficult for Drew and Rick to keep up the pace with their hands tied behind, and the Indian seemed to get great pleasure in jabbing them in the back with their bows when they stumbled.

The Yaqui camp was about a mile from where they had found Drew and Rick. Under normal conditions Drew could have run that distance in only a matter of minutes. But it took at least half an hour, due to stumbling, falling, and prodding.

The camp was totally different from Half Moon's. Instead of teepees the dwellings were low oval structures made of branches and limbs and covered with sod and mud. Fertile land, rather than vast desert, was covered with vegetation, and a river ran close-by. Drew couldn't believe that he was actually in an Indian camp.

The leader pulled his horse to a skidding stop before a low hogan at the edge of the camp. Sliding from the bare back of a chestnut mare, he stooped down and went in. Momentarily he emerged with a short stocky man who looked much as the first Indian did, only a little older.

Pointing a long brown finger at Nino Blanco and Money Man, then at Drew and Rick, the leader said something in a jumble of jerky words, shocking Drew when he actually smiled. Up until then, his face had been a stony mask of hatred. But now his features softened and white even teeth gleamed in the brown face. The older Indian nodded and the leader's smile broadened.

A thoughtful frown pulled more lines into the already wrinkled and weathered face of the older man. Drew was shocked even further when he suddenly smiled. But the smile faded fast as it had appeared when the leader and old man shifted their gaze from the horses to Drew and Rick. Naked hatred blazed in the leader's pale brown eyes again. The old man said something, turned abruptly, and went back inside the hogan.

The leader and the other Yaqui with the rifle came toward them, stopping a few feet away before moving around behind and giving them a hard push. They must have thought it was funny, because they burst out laughing.

Stumbling, Drew regained his balance as the Yaqui pushed him again. He wanted to whirl around and kick the living daylights out of the Indian, but common sense and self-preservation prevented him from doing it.

Apparently they were to be shown off as some kind of trophy, because they were led and pushed toward the main part of the camp. At a command from the leader, Yaquis of every size and shape formed two lines and watched the two white men as they walked through the camp. Unfriendly gestures and sounds followed them. Drew couldn't help but notice one little girl. She wasn't much bigger than the girl who'd helped them in Nogales. Her expression was different from the rest of the Indians. It was one of pity and sadness. Not hatred.

At the edge of the camp the leader, walking behind Drew, reached down, caught hold of the leather thong around Drew's wrists, and jerked hard. A hot streak of pain shot up Drew's arm and he fell back on the hard-packed ground. Black spots swam before his eyes again, and he wanted to vomit.

"You stinking, dirty bastard," Rick snarled, and before he thought of the consequences made a rush at the leader. But before he could reach him, the other Yaqui, holding the rifle, drew it back and let Rick have it right across the stomach. The impact doubled Rick over and he crumpled to his knees and fell facedown in the dirt. The Yaqui said something to the leader and they laughed boisterously.

Through a film of pain over his eyes, Drew looked at Rick and shook his head as Rick started getting up. He didn't want to say anything, believing that the sound of their voices only infuriated the Indians.

The Yaqui prodded them with the rifle barrel until they stood up. Then they were marched about a hundred yards from the camp to a clearing. Picking up four long sticks, the leader drove them into the hard-packed ground with a rock. Pushing Drew roughly down on the ground he pulled him backward, almost dragging him, took an extra leather thong, looped it over the one around Drew's wrists, then tied it to two of the sticks. The other Yaqui did the same with Rick. Then the six stood in single file in front of them and started laughing and pointing at them like a bunch of madmen.

The leader took the reins of Nino Blanco and the other brave took Money Man's reins. The two Indians swung up on their prizes and started back toward camp, turning around in the saddles to laugh again and point at the helpless men on the ground.

The scorching rays of the blazing sun beat down on them. Sweat ran from every pore like rivers and burned their eyes. The sweat burned like fire when it hit the cut on Drew's shoulder. Pain caused him to suck air through his teeth, which brought only more pain to his swollen lips.

"How long do you think they'll keep us here like this?" Rick asked in a whisper—although he could have yelled his head off if he'd wanted to, because there was no one around to hear him.

"I don't know," Drew answered, trying not to move his lips too much. Running the tip of his tongue around the inside of his mouth, he could feel the deep gash where his teeth had cut into his lips.

Drew had planned a slow revenge on Dayton for

what he'd done to Melissa and Little Moon. But the pain he was suffering just now made him know that if he could get his hands on Dayton right then, he'd kill him as fast as he could draw his gun from the holster.

"They might forget about us and let us roast in the sun," he went on, turning his head painfully to look at Rick. "Or they might come back, pour water on these leather thongs, and watch us bleed to death when the leather shrinks and cuts into our arms." A movement in the sky caught his attention and he looked up at four buzzards circling. "But they'll probably just let *them* take care of us."

Rick turned white when he looked up and saw the big black birds. "Up until now I really didn't have a quarrel with Dayton," he said in a tight voice, watching the buzzards drop lower, "but I promise you this: if I see him first, you won't have to lay a hand on him."

If Drew had felt like it, he would have laughed. "Can you move your hands?" he asked, trying to loosen the dry, hard stick driven deeply into the ground. He couldn't budge it!

"No," Rick answered, shaking his head and looking over at Drew. "Can you?" He took and expelled a deep, dejected breath when Drew shook his head.

"What are we going to do?" Rick asked, panic beginning to show in his voice. Drew didn't blame him. He was scared, too. This wasn't how he'd planned to spend his last days on earth. But that had been changed by the old man who'd led them into this trap.

"I don't know," Drew replied truthfully. "But think of how lucky we've been so far. Sanyo could have killed you—or me, for that matter—but he didn't. He even gave me a horse, a horse that I intend to get back and keep, by the way."

They both took encouragement from Drew's words, and for a little while were positive that things would work out for the best.

There had never been as long a day in Drew's life. The sun seemed to take forever to move only a little way in the bright blue sky. Judging from the shadows cast around them, it was around four when the leader rode out alone on Nino Blanco, a mocking grin on his brown face. The pale brown eyes smoldered in hatred. Dismounting, he checked Rick's hands, then moved slowly over to Drew, a threat in his narrowed eyes.

Stopping behind Drew, he bent down and tested the leather thong with a hard jerk on the stick. Once again he muttered something in the language Drew couldn't understand. Standing up, he kicked Drew as hard as he could in the center of his back. The breath left Drew's lungs in a painful swoosh and he knew he'd die before he could pull in some air. The leader walked slowly around in front of Drew and laughed mirthlessly down at him, then turned and walked toward Rick.

"When I get my hands untied," Drew grated between clenched teeth—and knowing what the consequences would be from speaking out, certain that the Indian was going to kill him, he rushed on as the leader came back toward him, walking slowly like a cat stalking its prey, his hate-filled eyes never leaving Drew's face—"I swear I'm going to cut you up in little pieces and feed you to those buzzards!"

As Drew's last words were spoken the leader bent down and slapped him as hard as he could across the face with the back of his hand. Taking satisfaction when blood ran down Drew's cheek, the Yaqui smiled slightly, got back on the white horse, and rode off at a fast gallop, sitting straight and proud on the worn saddle.

"If you say one more thing to that savage, he'll kill you," Rick pointed out solemnly, disbelief narrowing his eyes. "What does he have against you? The sound of your voice makes him crazy."

Drew's face felt six times bigger than it should have as he shook his head. His mouth throbbed and his shoulder burned like fire.

"I don't know," he replied, leaning back to take some of the pressure off his arms. "But when I get loose I'm going to kill him. Then I'm going after Dayton. That old man's going to curse the day he was born."

"You'll have to beat me to him first," Rick said with a snort.

Shadows lengthened as the sun began sliding down behind the mountains. The land started cooling, and Drew and Rick's shirts dried and were stiff with sweat and body salt. They shivered in the chilly breeze.

"Have you loosened your hands any?" Drew asked, trying to undo the strips of leather that were beginning to cut into the flesh. He knew the sticky moisture he could feel wasn't sweat but his own blood.

"No," Rick replied, pulling at the leather. "Your buddy knows how to tie a good knot." He chuckled at his own dry humor. "Something just struck me," he went on seriously, all the joking gone from his voice.

"If Dayton was close enough for us to see him—and then not long after these kick-happy Indians got us—why do you suppose they didn't want him?"

In the dim light Drew saw a tight frown on Rick's face. It pulled deep lines between his brows. Suddenly the thought that had been in the back of his mind popped to the surface.

"Where did those two Indians get Winchesters?" he asked, staring down at his boots, then over at Rick.

Rick leaned toward Drew as far as his bound hands would allow. His eyes widened as Drew's question hit him.

"Are you thinking what I think you are?" Rick asked, squinting his eyes in the dimness. He grinned slightly when Drew nodded.

"Now I know what Dayton meant when he said something about good hunting to that waiter in Nogales," Drew answered, his thoughts momentarily sidetracked away from his present dilemma. "I'll bet you my last dime that Dayton's giving guns to these Indians just like his lousy sons were to Half Moon. He led us to them as an added little bonus."

He bit off his last word as a soft sound, just loud enough to be called a sound, reached his ears. Something or somebody was moving behind them in the weeds. His heart slammed up into his throat as he listened harder to the nearing sound. Somebody was walking and trying to be careful. Whoever it was either hadn't done this very often or was the most clumsy human alive.

"Do you hear that?" Drew asked in a whisper. His mouth went dry and his breath reached only halfway to his lungs.

"Yeah," Rick answered. "Is it man or animal?" Drew wanted to laugh, but hearing only seriousness in Rick's voice, didn't.

"We'll soon find out," Drew answered, feeling something brushing against his hands. Turning around as far as his bound hands would allow, he was startled to see the small girl who'd been watching them so sadly when they'd been marched through the camp.

He was surprised even more when he saw the girl take a knife from her pocket, the long blade reflecting the moon just coming up over the mountains.

Had the leader sent a girl to kill them? Was this some kind of test or challenge for her? He'd never heard of any bravery test or challenges for girls. Those tests were usually reserved for only boys. Was this a final insult? For them to be killed by a little girl? Drew's heart almost stopped.

But his fears were put to rest when he felt the cold blade against his wrist. In one swift motion the leather thong fell away. His arms were so stiff from being in one position so long that they felt like they'd break off at the joint, and the cut in his shoulder began burning like fire again as the movement opened the cut.

"If you can, grab her," Drew said quickly, easing his right arm around with his left hand. The girl apparently didn't understand English, because she kept moving over toward Rick.

It took no longer to free Rick than it did Drew, and as the leather thong fell away Rick spun around, grabbed the girl around the waist, and clamped his hand over her mouth.

The girl's surprised scream was muffled under Rick's broad hand. Her arms and legs flailed wildly about, but Rick kept his arm tight around her.

Crawling quickly over to Rick and the girl, Drew caught her hand and began gently patting it. Both Drew and Rick were surprised when she calmed down a little, but her brown eyes were wide in fear. For some reason she tightened her small hand around Drew's.

Going on a hunch, Drew put his finger across his lips and blew through his teeth. The girl stared at Drew for a second then nodded her black head. Rick moved his hand but kept it close.

"Do you know English?" Drew whispered, bending close to the girl. He couldn't believe it when she nodded slowly and smiled. How had she learned it and who had taught her? Something in the back of his mind told him he wouldn't like the answer to the question.

"Why did you help us?" Drew asked, curiosity eating at him. What she had done could get her into serious trouble or killed.

"I hear old one tell Chihara you coming," the girl answered in uncertain English. Chihara must be the one Drew had thought of as the leader.

"How often does the old one come here?" Drew asked slowly. He knew he was wasting time with these questions, but something told him he'd be glad to know later.

"Every time moon is full," the girl answered simply, standing up. She didn't try to run or call out. She glanced uncertainly from Drew to Rick.

"How long does the old one stay?" Drew asked,

peering closely at the girl in the moonlight. Then he remembered the rifle. "Does the old one bring anything when he comes?"

When she hesitated for a second, Drew thought she had gotten scared and didn't want to tell him anything else.

"Old one not stay long," she finally said, taking a deep breath. "Sometimes, not this time, he brings long guns."

So Dayton *was* supplying the Yaquis with rifles. Drew wasn't really that surprised.

"Did old one teach you English?" he asked. She nodded.

"Can you get us to our horses?" Rick asked, standing up and kicking his legs to get the kinks out. The girl nodded again.

"Are you going to get into trouble for helping us?" Drew asked, struggling to his feet. The girl shook her head. Rubbing his right arm, he winced when he hit the cut. It felt hard and hot. He knew it needed attention but that would have to wait. They had to get away.

By now the moon was a silver ball high in the sky, throwing a light over everything. They had to hurry before Chihara came to check on them.

The girl started walking back the way she'd come, then stopped and waited for them to follow, an anxious expression in her large eyes.

"If we get the horses first," Rick asked in a nervous whisper, falling into step with Drew behind the girl, "what do you plan to do with Chihara?"

Drew jerked around and looked at Rick in the moonlight. He was caught off guard by the question and didn't have an answer ready. He knew he owed Chihara more than one, but wasn't sure what to do. But if what the girl said was true, Chihara was only doing what Caleb Dayton had told him to do.

Chihara had only captured Drew and Rick in order to give Dayton more time to get farther away. The additional kicks, pushes, and slaps had been for his own satisfaction.

"I'll tell you what," Drew whispered across the short distance. "If we can only get to the horses and leave out of here without any more trouble, I'm willing to forget about Chihara and just go after Dayton." The frown told him what was in Rick's mind. "I know what you're thinking," Drew went on, "but this kid could get into lots of trouble if we hang around here very long."

"Yeah, I see your point," Rick agreed sullenly. "We've got to find our guns, too."

Drew reached out and caught the girl's shoulders, stopping her. She turned around, fear on her brown face, her eyes big.

"Do you know where our guns are?" Drew asked, bending down so his voice wouldn't carry over the quiet night.

He was puzzled when the girl nodded and smiled slightly. How could this child—and a girl, at that—know so much about what went on in the camp? Most children this age were only interested in playing. And girls usually didn't know the first thing about camp matters.

The girl motioned for them to follow her, and they made eerie shadows in the moonlight as they crept along.

It took longer to get back to the actual camp, because they were trying to be quiet and careful and weren't being dragged along. Rounding a boulder that was still warm to the touch, they stopped short.

Chihara, the old Indian, and the other five warriors were sitting on the ground in a circle around a small fire. They were passing a jug of something around, and judging from their laughter and slurred voices, it wasn't water or milk.

Chihara was slouched back against a rock, his arms lying limp at his side, his mouth open and slack-jawed. His eyes were closed. The older Indian was mumbling a chant and wagging his head back and forth. The other five were in various stages of being drunk and were no threat to them.

"This way," the girl urged, reaching out and tapping Drew's arm. Without taking any chances, the girl stepped back a couple of feet and began moving almost silently toward a low hogan. Drew was stunned when she walked straight into it without even pausing to see if it was safe to enter.

In a matter of seconds she returned with both Drew's and Rick's pistols and rifles. When she handed the guns to Drew there was a slight smile on the brown face. Drew had never thought it would be this simple! Somebody up there was really on their side. It was almost too good to be true.

The girl waved her arm a little frantically for them to follow, and she led the way to the back of the camp where all of the horses were tied. Money Man and Nino Blanco were tied but not hobbled at the edge of the remuda. If I were Chihara, Drew thought, and had two prize horses like these, I'd have put them in a more secure place. Both horses had been unsaddled but were still wearing bridles. Taking precious time to saddle the horses, Drew and Rick swung up and looked down at the girl. She smiled at them a pleased glow on her upturned face.

"Are you sure you won't get into any trouble with Chihara because of this?" Drew asked, reaching down and patting the girl's head. He was worried about what would happen to her after the Yaquis sobered up and found them gone.

"No," she answered with a short laugh. "Chihara my father." She laughed at the shocked expression on Drew's face.

"Your father?" he questioned louder than he intended. "Did he put you up to helping us? Does he know you were going to do it?"

The girl shook her head without saying anything. Drew guessed that answered both questions. He knew they were testing fate in talking to the girl, but he had one more question to ask although she'd told him part of what he wanted to know earlier. He wanted to see if the child's answer would be the same.

"Where did your father get that rifle?" He wasn't surprised.

"Old one give gun," she replied, repeating what she'd said before. With another laugh she turned and ran back the way they'd just come.

Kneeing the horses in the side they took off at a fast gallop, hoping the Yaqui would stay drunk for a long time.

Dayton had a good head start on them, but wouldn't be aware of the fact that Chihara's daughter had helped them escape. Maybe he'd stop somewhere along the way and rest. Drew knew the chances of that happening was like rock turning to sugar.

Following the riverbed that ran north of the camp, they stopped once to refill the canteens with fresh cool water. The tall canebrakes on either side of the river eventually gave way to cactus and rocks.

The moonlight on the cactus arms, turned every which direction, transformed them into grotesque figures. Howling coyotes and hooting owls sent shivers up and down their backs and arms. They knew they were being watched, but weren't sure if by men or beasts or Caleb Dayton. To Drew, Dayton was just like his sons. Less than a human and less than an animal.

The horses were rested, and wanting to cover as much ground as possible the men let them run in the cool night air. When the horses' burst of energy was spent they stopped by a small stream, loosened the saddles, and stretched out on the bare ground and slept until the sounds of a puma growling in the rocks above them drove the sleep abruptly away. Dawn was just dividing the earth from the sky, anyway, and the men knew they had a long way to go and a lot to do before finding Caleb Dayton.

"If that old devil's been coming down here often," Drew said over his shoulder to Rick as they tightened the cinches, "and giving guns to Chihara and the others, he probably knows every rock, pebble, and crevice in these mountains." Hatred and irritation edged his voice. "It's going to be hard to find him."

Rick stopped what he was doing and looked at Drew over the saddle. Drew's mouth was tight and his eyes were narrow.

"You're not suggesting we stop looking for him, are you?" he asked. Anger snapped in his blue eyes and his chest rose and fell in short breaths. He hated to think that he'd been beaten up and tied to a stake like an animal for nothing.

"Lord, no!" Drew snapped, jerking his head up, his eyes dark in a frown. His mouth popped open in surprise. "After what he's put us through! Are you crazy? I just meant that he knows this country a whole heck of a lot better than we do, and it will take a lot of luck on our part to find him. Why would you think that I'd give up looking for him?"

"Nothing, really," Rick answered, arching his brows. "I don't mind so much not taking care of that Indian back there. You were the one he was using for a punching bag. But Dayton's the one who got us into all of this and I'd sure hate like the devil to lose my chance at him!"

In a gesture that was unlike him, Rick gave the cinch a savage yank that brought Money Man's head around to look at him. Surprise was almost visible in the horse's brown eyes. Rick patted his head and rubbed between his eyes.

"Oh, believe me," Drew said, a snide smile on his unshaven face, his eyes narrow, "you won't lose your chance at Caleb Dayton. You're just going to have to wait in line a long time behind me to do it, that's all."

They rode until the sun was directly overhead and beating down on them. Their shirts were wet and sticking to their backs.

"I wonder how long this Dayton's been giving guns to these Indians?" Drew commented wearily, pulling back on the reins and dismounting under a cottonwood tree. The clear river that had run through the Yaqui camp eased over shallow rocks and they decided to rest out the sun for a while. They unsaddled the horses after they'd been watered.

Flopping down against the trunk of the tree, Drew reached up tentatively to rub his right shoulder. He flinched at the light touch and moaned in pain. His arm felt like fire. Rick, hearing the sound, turned around and was shocked at the pale and sick look on Drew's drawn face.

"Are you all right?" he asked, taking a canteen from the saddle horn and squatting down beside Drew. He could tell at once from the tight lines around Drew's mouth that his cousin was far from all right.

"I would be, if the fire in my shoulder would go out," Drew replied weakly, pushing off his hat and leaning his head against the tree. His eyes closed slowly and opened.

"Let's have a look," Rick suggested, leaning closer and taking a sharp knife from his pocket. Drew's face contorted in pain when Rick pulled the dried blood and torn shirt away. In two swift motions the dirty shirt sleeve was eased down Drew's arm and discarded on the ground.

Rick opened the canteen and poured water up on Drew's shoulder to let it run over the cut, which seemed to look a lot worse than it was. But when the caked blood had been washed away, Rick realized that the cut was bad. A small piece of rock was imbedded in the half-inch gash, and several strands of cloth were hanging from it. The flesh around the cut was bright red and swollen.

"How does it look?" Drew questioned shakily, twisting his head around to see. Closing his eyes he swallowed and leaned his head back.

"Worse than I thought," Rick replied truthfully, squinting his eyes and shaking his head, "but not as bad as it could be. There's a piece of rock in there that has to come out. I'll try not to hurt you too much."

"You couldn't hurt me much more than that does," Drew said in a low voice, inclining his head sideways.

Rick knew the knife should be sterilized before working on Drew's arm, but he didn't want to waste the time building a fire, so he did the next best thing. Getting up, he struck a match and ran the flame up and down the blade. He knelt down by Drew and felt sorry for what he was about to do.

"Wish I had something to give you," Rick said remorsefully, a wan smile on his face. "I could hit you in the jaw," he went on with a short laugh.

"Just do it," Drew said softly, pressing his lips tightly together and shutting his eyes. He was gritting his teeth so hard against the impending pain that knots stood out in both sides of his jaws.

Taking hold of the ends of the cloth, Rick pulled them loose and blood began dripping out. He could see the rock and thought it would be easy to just put the tip of the knife blade behind it and flip it out. But that wasn't to be the case. The rock was bigger on the imbedded side than he'd thought.

Gripping the knife tighter in his hand, Rick inserted it further into the gash. He could feel and hear the blade scraping against the rock. The sound sent chills up and down his own back.

Drew moaned in pain and gritted his teeth harder. Sweat popped out on his pale face and his head fell back against the tree.

"Sorry," Rick muttered, swallowing hard and taking a deep breath. "I'm almost through. Hang on just a little longer."

Drew looked up at him, exasperation and pain in his eyes.

"It's got to come out, Drew," Rick said, catching his top lip between his teeth. He stood up to relax his legs, then squatted down again. "If it isn't gotten out, your arm could rot off."

A weak smile spread across Drew's face and he swallowed hard. "All right," he relented, nodding slowly. "I can't go after Dayton with a rotten arm." He took a deep breath and held it.

Rick allowed a hearty laugh to relieve some of his tenseness, then leaned over Drew's shoulder with the knife. He was amazed at how steady his hand was. He'd never done this sort of thing before.

Pain such as Drew had never before experienced rushed over him like a tide when Rick started digging again. His arm had never hurt this bad when Tom Dayton had shot him. He remembered how Melissa had petted and coddled him after Dr. Bryan had cleaned the wound and dressed it.

Her cool, soft fingers didn't hurt anymore as she probed for the bullet . . . No, his mind tried to say. There was no bullet. That was some time ago. This thing in his shoulder was sharp and something burned like a poker. But she was there. He knew she was.

"It's all right, Drew," Melissa whispered against his

ear. Her honey-colored hair brushed his cheek. Drew's brain tried to tell him things weren't right here, but those things just wouldn't take shape and hold. He could see her and that's all that mattered. If he'd had the strength to raise his arms he could have held her again. But they were too heavy.

"It doesn't hurt much, Melissa," he could hear himself saying. "You're here now."

"Drew. Drew. It's over. The rock's out." The voice was soft and gentle, then became deep and serious. A thin haze clouded Drew's vision, and two faces, Melissa's and Rick's, floated back and forth in his thinking.

"Drew, can you hear me?" This time there was no mistaking Rick's deep voice. Drew blinked his eyes several times, and that helped clear his vision. He felt alone and lost when he looked up to see that it was only Rick's bearded face leaning over him. He couldn't understand why he was lying on the ground instead of leaning against the tree as he had been.

"What happened?" he asked in a low voice. "Did you push me over?" Bracing his left hand on the grass, he forced himself up and sagged against the tree.

"No, I didn't push you over," Rick answered pensively, standing up and walking over to the white horse and opening the saddlebag. Pulling out a clean blue shirt he came back to Drew and squatted down. "Would you believe you passed out? You kept mumbling something about Melissa." He handed Drew the shirt and avoided his eyes.

"How long was I out?" Drew asked, rolling to his knees and then struggling to his feet. He felt so lonely it was hard not to cry, and he had to blink his eyes not to do so.

"Not very long," Rick answered, wrinkling his forehead and squinting his eyes. "Maybe ten minutes. I got the rock out." He pitched the white rock across the short distance and Drew caught it in his left hand. The backside, which had been imbedded so deep in his arm, was jagged and had a small hook on the end.

"No wonder you passed out," Rick went on, wanting to get Drew's mind off Melissa. He realized that the desolate expression in Drew's eyes had nothing to do with the pain in his arm, that the brief time Drew had been unconscious he'd been with Melissa again. "I really had some deep digging to do to get it out."

Drew lowered his head and looked down at the shirt as if he'd never seen it before. He felt silly that he'd passed out—no, call it what it really was— fainted from some pain. He wondered how much pain Melissa had suffered before she died. He knew in his mind that it had to have been a lot worse than the cut on his arm. The thought of how she must have looked caused his stomach to turn over, and he knew he was going to be sick.

Spinning around with his back to Rick, he doubled over and let the bitter contents of his stomach spill from his throat. When it was over he stumbled to the river, stripped off his clothes and boots, and sank down in the cool and refreshing water. He tried to tell himself that the water drops on his cheeks were from washing his face, but in reality he knew they were tears. Drew was glad that he had his back to Rick.

He stayed in the river until the dirt, sweat, blood, and misery were washed away. Coming out of the water he found a pair of pants and socks on the bank. After he'd dressed, he walked over to where Rick was sitting by the small fire. Rick had made coffee and flat bread and Drew discovered that he was hungry. As he ate, a question kept nagging at him and he had to know.

"Rick," he began hesitantly, staring down into the steaming cup of coffee, "you said that I talked about Melissa. What did I say?" He felt foolish in asking.

"Oh, nothing really," Rick answered, breaking off a piece of bread and chewing it. "Just that something didn't hurt very much. I don't know what you were talking about, 'cause the way I was cutting into your arm had to hurt like the devil. Don't worry about it. We all do what we need to in order to make it."

Pain that had nothing to do with his arm pulled at Drew's heart again. Unable to help it, though, a small smile eased across his mouth.

"No, it wasn't that," he replied softly. "I guess I was talking about the time when Dayton shot me in the shoulder. Melissa fussed over me like an old mother hen." Drew had to stop talking. His chin started quivering and tears stung his eyes.

Rick's feelings were a mixture of embarrassment at watching a man reveal a weaker side of his emotions because of a woman and sympathy because a man had lost a wife he obviously loved very much, not to mention a child he would never watch grow up.

"You cared for her a lot, didn't you?" Rick didn't look at Drew. He just turned the coffee cup round and round in his big hands.

The question, and the stupidity of it, caught Drew off guard. Snapping his head up he stared at Rick.

He wanted to lash out at his cousin for his insensitivity but didn't when he realized that Rick had never been in his boots.

"I never thought I'd care for a woman as much as I did her." Drew nodded slowly and smiled again. The ache in his heart was as painful as the knife in his shoulder when Rick had been digging out the rock.

Rick felt silly and wished he hadn't asked such a dumb question.

For a while they sat quietly, each lost in his own thoughts.

"Well," Rick said abruptly, slapping his hands down against his thighs and standing up, "I feel as dirty as a pig up to his armpits in mud, so I think I'll take a bath." Taking a set of clean clothes from the saddlebags he went to the river, stripped, and sank down in the waist-deep water. After he'd bathed, washed his hair, and dressed, he sat down by Drew under the tree.

"Why don't we spend the night here?" he suggested, stretching his long legs out and crossing them at the ankles. "You'll feel more like traveling tomorrow and we can make better time."

Drew was glad Rick had suggested it. He didn't want him to get the idea that he couldn't cope with something as mundane as a wounded shoulder. But suddenly everything that had happened to them over the past few days caught up with him, and all of his energy ebbed away and he felt like an old rag.

"You're right," he agreed, getting up and taking the bedroll and kicking it out. "How fast can that mule go, anyway?" They both laughed.

Stretching out on the blanket, Drew hoped that

he'd feel better tomorrow as he watched the yellow sun slide down behind the mountains. Lavender, pink, and orange streaks colored the blue sky. A few white cottonball-like clouds skimmed easily along. As the sun dropped, so did the temperature. Sleep soon closed their eyes and they were that much closer to catching up with Caleb Dayton.

Chapter VI

Drew was awakened the next morning by a tickling on his arm. There was enough light from the dawn just breaking over the mountains for him to see an at-least-three-inch dark brown scorpion easing up his arm toward his elbow. The stinger was curled down, ready to strike. With his thumb and middle finger he thumped it away and then shivered, the hairs on his arm seeming to stand up.

Again a mental image of Caleb Dayton being tied down and tortured, this time by scorpions crawling all over him, flashed through Drew's mind and he grinned.

"No," he said softly but out loud. "Caleb Dayton's so mean that if all of the scorpions in the desert stung him they'd probably die from his poison."

The grin stayed on his face, though, as he got to his feet and put on his hat—after checking to see if there were any more inhabitants inside.

"Who were you talking to?" Rick asked, getting up and rolling his blankets together.

"No one, really," Drew answered, swinging his right arm to test its soreness. A pain shot all the way to his fingers and his eyes smarted. "There was a scorpion on my arm a while ago, and I was just thinking about Dayton being tied down and a bunch of them crawling all over him."

"I'm glad I'm with you, Drew," Rick said, grimacing as he poured water into the coffeepot. "I'd hate to be against you. You have some wild ideas."

"That's mild in comparison to what I'm going to do to Dayton when I get my hands on him." Drew's voice was level and threatening and his blue eyes were cold.

"How does your arm feel?" Rick asked, adding coffee to the fresh water in the pot. Then he took meat from the grub sack.

"Well," Drew answered, shaking his head as though dispelling the morbid thoughts from his mind. "I can't wrestle a mountain lion, but it feels a heck of a lot better than it did yesterday. Now it won't rot off."

Hearty laughter burst from Rick. Drew grinned at him. Rick stirred flour and water together, poured it into the pan, then put it on the fire. After the bread was done they sliced it, put the meat between it, and washed it all down with the strong coffee.

"Well," Drew said, dashing the remains of coffee on the fire and standing up, "let's saddle up and go after Dayton."

His lips were pressed together and his expression was determined. Picking up the utensils he took them to the river and washed them.

By the time the sun had cleared the mountain tops, Drew and Rick had saddled the horses and gathered up their gear. The land soon changed from grassy flat to dry desert. As they rode along, they looked down at the ground for any sign of horse tracks. They didn't find any, and soon they would be out of Mexico.

"Do you have the feeling that we're being watched again?" Drew asked, glancing at his cousin.

Was Chihara following them? Drew wondered how the Yaqui had felt when he sobered up and found them gone. Had the little girl gotten into trouble because of them? Drew prayed that she hadn't.

The watching eyes could be bandits or federal troops. But Drew knew it was Dayton.

"I was just going to ask you the same thing," Rick replied, dropping his hand down to the pistol handle.

"We'll be all right as soon as we get across the border," Drew encouraged. Just the same, he loosened the Colt .45 in the holster after checking the shells in the rifle.

A breath of relief swooshed out of them as they crossed a section of ground that they imagined to be the dividing line between Mexico and Arizona.

About a hundred yards from the border they saw an oak tree. That in itself wasn't the disturbing thing. The long dark object swinging from a limb was what got Drew's attention as he started to dismount.

"What in the devil is that?" he asked Rick, drawing the words out and swinging his leg back over the saddle and sitting there motionless.

"If I didn't know better, I'd swear it's a dead body," Rick answered, his eyes drawn together in thin slits as he strained to see better. His mouth gaped open. Kicking the horses in the sides, they covered the distance in a matter of seconds.

Hot anger raced through Drew when they reached the tree. He knew that he'd been made a fool of again! Rick's "dead body" was a dangling black slicker. A jagged piece of paper was folded twice, and a small hole punched in it so it would fit over a button.

Drew rode directly up to the slicker, disgust etched all over his face. Even before he took the paper down, he knew who it was from. His hands shook in anger as he jerked the paper down, opened it, and read the crude words.

Wilums, them Injuns outa kiled ye. I thot they wud. I cud hav twis. Ye won no whur I am. Yel pa fer merder.

"Don't tell me that's from Dayton," Rick said in disbelief, pulling Money Man over closer to Drew.

"Okay, I won't," Drew growled, sucking his mouth in against teeth and handing Rick the paper.

"How long ago do you think he left this?" Rick asked wearily, swallowing hard and looking around at the rocks in the distance.

"Hard to tell," Drew answered, feeling the hairs stand out on the back of his neck. He knew beyond a shadow of a doubt that Dayton was watching them. The note couldn't have been written and left too long ago, and for two reasons: They really hadn't lost that much time in following Dayton even though they'd stopped early because of Drew's arm, and Dayton wouldn't have taken the chance of a strong wind coming up and blowing it away.

Dayton was probably watching them at that very minute and laughing at them. Drew was right. Dayton had made a fool of them again!

Kneeing the horse in the side Drew rode a wide circle around the tree, and was more than surprised to see two sets of hoofprints heading north. The prints weren't very far apart, so that meant Dayton hadn't been in any hurry to get where he was going. He probably had it in his mind to stay just a little way ahead of them and pick them off when it suited him.

"Rick, this way," Drew called out, kicking the horse in the side and following the clear tracks.

"We're like fish in a barrel," Rick pointed out in a tight voice, pulling his rifle from the scabbard and laying it across his legs.

"I know," Drew acknowledged with a nod. "But not right now. Dayton is playing a game of hide and lead with us. I will admit that I've never come across a man as crafty and sly as he is."

Rick pulled his hat lower on his head and looked sideways at Drew. He couldn't understand why Drew was so calm. Or was that just an outward attitude?

Drew wasn't scared; just worried and angered. If Dayton had really had the chance to kill him and Rick — and with such a vengeance driving him — why hadn't he done it and gotten it over with? Last night would have been another ideal chance.

"Well, I don't know about you," Drew said slowly and evenly, sucking his lip in against his teeth, "but I'm getting tired of playing Dayton's games. Let's go!"

Kicking the horses in the side they followed the prints which seemed to go on and on.

They'd covered several miles when a cloud of dust and a rumbling noise stopped them. When they crested a hill, Drew couldn't believe his eyes!

Below, at least five hundred head of cattle were running as fast as their legs could carry them. Riders spurred their horses as fast as the cattle were going, but the cattle were out of control.

One rider, looking up for any number of reasons, saw them and motioned frantically for them to come down.

"Seems those boys could use a little help," Drew said placidly, surprising Rick with both the offer and the levity in his voice.

"What about Dayton?" Rick questioned, raising his brows.

"Dayton will be there tomorrow," Drew answered, raising his voice to be heard over the noise of the stampeding cattle.

Kneeing Nino Blanco in the side, Drew raced down the hill, Rick and Money Man right on his heels.

The man who'd been riding to the left of the herd and who'd waved to them came at a fast gallop.

"I don't know what spooked 'um," he said in short breaths, sweat rolling down his weathered brown face, pulling the horse to a short stop. "If I lose that herd, Jessie Wallace will have my butt." Drew read truth and worry in the tired gray eyes.

"Why would you lose the herd?" Drew asked impatiently, watching the mass of horns and hoofs roar on.

"There's a drop-off about two miles ahead," the rider explained quickly, removing a battered hat and wiping his hand up over his forehead and damp reddish brown hair. "The cows in front will see it and should be able to stop. But those following will shove them over." Anxiety showed in his eyes, and catching his underlip between tobacco-stained teeth, he shook his head disdainfully.

"Well, let's stop wasting our time," Drew said

impatiently. Pulling his hat down tighter, he reached back and untied the bedroll, removed the yellow slicker, rerolled and tied the bedroll.

"They have a good head start," the man said, replacing his battered brown hat. "Why don't both of you take the left flank and try turning them north as soon as you reach the point. Your horses seem well rested and can make better time than mine can. Look for a guy wearing a green hat. His name's Bush Waggoner and he was riding point. Good luck. I think you're going to need it. By the way, I'm John Cameron."

Reaching over he extended his hand, and Drew did likewise. "Drew Williams," he introduced, then indicated his thumb toward Rick. "This is my cousin, Rick Gregston. We'll see you when this is over."

Kneeing the horses into quick movement and swinging wide left, it didn't take Nino Blanco's and Money Man's long and sturdy legs to cover a good portion of ground. Whatever had spooked the cattle had done a good job. They were running at breakneck speed, not knowing or caring what was ahead of them. The air was filled with the roar of thundering hoofs, bellowing sounds, and choking dust.

At first Drew thought it was strange that no riders were visible, but he soon realized that they must all be up near the head of the stampeding cattle.

Dust that choked the nose and stung the eyes filled the air, and Drew pulled his bandanna up over his face. That helped some but didn't keep it out of his eyes. Squinting only helped a little.

Time and distance were both running out, and at the speed the cattle were going it wouldn't take long for them to reach the drop-off.

Leaning forward in the saddle, Drew put his heels to Nino Blanco again. The big horse seemed to leap ahead and the long strides ate up the ground, clods of dirt dug up by the mighty hoofs.

Looking over his shoulder Drew saw Rick and Money Man right behind him. Rick had swung out his lariat and was waving it wildly over his head.

Straightening up in the saddle, Drew rode as fast as Nino Blanco would go and as close to the cattle as he dared. He began waving the slicker over his head and actually flapping it against the cow's side. Catching sight of the motions, the cows began crowding in to the right. Drew suddenly wondered how he and Rick had gotten into this mess.

Oh, well, he thought grimly, mentally shrugging his shoulders, this entire trip has been full of unexpected events so why should this particular instance be any different?

He was a little angered, though, that he and Rick had more or less been volunteered for this. They'd lost two days indirectly because of Dayton, and it was directly because of Dayton that they were helping John Cameron save this herd for his boss.

Nino Blanco's hoof struck a large rock and the big horse lost the rhythm of motion momentarily and he stumbled, bringing Drew's thoughts back to the business at hand. Nino Blanco regained his balance and they raced on.

Drew wasn't sure how much ground had been covered but knew he was getting closer to the front of the herd because he could see four riders and the herd seemed to be turning north. Various sounds, catcalls, whoops, and whistles filled the air. Snorts, bellows, and howls intermingled with the other sounds. Through the dust he spotted the green hat belonging to Bush Waggoner. Just as Drew saw the green hat he got the sensation that he was falling.

Jerking around in the saddle he glanced to the left and saw that he was at the edge of the drop-off! Pulling roughly on the reins Drew tried to keep the horse upright, but it was too late. Nino Blanco's hoofs couldn't find sure footing, and amid rocks and dirt they tumbled at least a hundred feet down the drop-off. The horse screamed in terror. Drew was thrown from the saddle, and landed with such a thud that the breath was knocked out of him. Somehow he managed to hang onto the reins. Suddenly he remembered falling in the sandstorm just outside of Tucson on his way back to Fort Rather.

Nino Blanco struggled to his feet, his eyes wild, and he snorted the dirt from his flared nostrils. For a nervous moment Drew sat on the ground. He was afraid to take a breath, knowing he'd broken something by hitting so many rocks on the way down.

"Drew, are you all right?" Drew turned his head slowly at the urgent call in Rick's voice, and nodded. Bracing his weight on one knee he got to his feet and swung up into the saddle. Kneeing the horse in the side, they climbed the drop-off with much more effort than it had taken to get down.

Reaching the top he dismounted and rubbed his left knee. There was already an ache in it.

Bush Waggoner came riding toward them, removing the dirty green hat and wiping his face.

"Are ye sure ye be all right, young fellow?" Drew's

head snapped up at the strange accent. He'd never heard one like it before. Pale blue eyes regarded him with concern and amusement. "Ye mighta cracked yer skull."

"Yes," Drew replied dejectedly, nodding slowly. "I'm all right." Then he dropped his head. He wanted to laugh. The man's thick red hair stood up like a porcupine's. Drew knew why he was called "Bush." Self-consciously the man clamped the hat back on, then grinned at Drew.

"It does be lookin' a bit of a mess, now, doesn't it?" Waggoner said. Peering down closer at Drew, the older man squinted his blue eyes. "Ye not be one of the regulars. Who are ye?"

Drew introduced himself and Rick, and in a few words explained why they were there.

"Well, let's don't be dawdling," Waggoner said impatiently, taking up the reins. "It's a long way we've got to be goin'." He took off in a burst of speed and was soon lost in the dust.

Whether it was the distance or the persistent riders pressing into the herd with the noise they were making, the cattle began turning and slowing.

John Cameron, followed by two riders, brought in a dozen strays. The three men looked as tired as Drew and Rick felt.

"I've never been through anything like that before," Cameron said, puzzled, taking a long breath and expelling it through the wide space between his front teeth. He shook his head. "I don't mean that I've never been in a stampede before, but usually there's an obvious reason for it. Lightning or a sudden movement. But there's nothing out there." He waved his arm in a sweeping motion to indicate the quiet vastness.

Listening to Cameron talk, Drew got a funny feeling in the pit of his stomach. "What do you mean 'usually'?" he asked slowly, lowering his head and squinting his eyes.

"Well, any unexpected noise will set cattle off," Cameron explained slowly, throwing his head back and reveling in his knowledge. "But this time I didn't hear anything." He pulled his mouth into a smug line against his teeth and shook his head.

One of the two riders with Cameron wiped his face with a bandanna and rode nearer Cameron.

"John," he said, pushing back his hat, "there was a loud bang just before the herd took off."

"What kind of bang did you hear?" The question burst from Drew before he was aware of it. Something told him he already knew the answer. Had Dayton hoped that he and Rick would be trampled by the cattle?

"Well," the rider began wrinkling his forehead and scratching a growth of thick black beard, "it sounded like a shotgun to me. Right after that, the herd stampeded."

John Cameron whirled around in the saddle, a frown on his weathered face. Drew knew from the frown on Cameron's face that he didn't like being corrected in front of strangers.

"Skaggs, you've been out in the sun too long," Cameron accused, glaring at the rider. "When could you have heard a shotgun? There hasn't been anyone around here with a shotgun in a long time. We all carry rifles and pistols."

Skaggs broke off a chunk of tobacco, put it into his mouth, and wiggled it over to the right side of his jaw.

"Oh, it wasn't none of us," he explained, shaking his head rapidly. "It was . . ."

Here it comes, Drew thought, feeling rage and anger boil over him. He noticed that he was breathing hard.

"Let me tell you who it was," Drew said slowly, his eyes snapping, his voice bringing all heads in his direction. "It was an old man wearing a floppy black hat and riding a mule. He was leading a horse. My horse. His name's Caleb Dayton. What you heard wasn't a shotgun. It was a Sharps .54 buffalo gun."

"You're right," Skaggs agreed, looking at him as if he were crazy. His mouth gaped open. "How did you know?"

"We've been after that old rattlesnake for almost a week now," Rick answered, looking questioningly at Drew. Rick was surprised at his own answer.

"Who's this Dayton to you?" Cameron asked, turning back to Drew, a deep frown between his brows. "Why would he stampede this herd?" His eyes narrowed while he waited for Drew to explain.

In as few as possible words, although he'd told it so many times that he sounded rehearsed, Drew told about the Dayton brothers, Melissa, the Indians, and finally Caleb Dayton.

John Cameron, Skaggs, and the other rider listened in rapt awe as Drew recounted the happenings of the past year.

"Why in the world haven't you killed that worthless scum before now?" Cameron asked, squinting his eyes and frowning in exasperation.

"Well," Drew said, letting the word strain out, feeling stupid—if that was what Cameron implied—that a man of his age, strength, and experience had been outwitted by an old buffalo hider who rode a mule. "The old coot's always managed to be an inch ahead of us every step of the way. The nearest we've been to him was a couple of days ago just before the Yaqui Indians got us."

Judging from the shocked look on Cameron's face, Drew knew he'd left out some of his explanation.

"Yaqui Indians?" Cameron repeated, lowering his head a little and cocking a brow at Drew. "Don't tell me that crazy Chihara had you." Astonishment enlarged his eyes. "Boy, if you managed to get away from that savage—and I mean that very word—you're one lucky son of a gun." Cameron shook his head in dismay and admiration.

"I guess we're that lucky, then," Drew said, pressing his lips together and smiling.

"I want to hear how you did it," Cameron said, pulling his hat lower over his eyes. "The boss will, too. So I guess we'd better get these cattle moving again. We're supposed to meet them at Leaning Rock Crossing."

Swinging the horse around and kicking it in the side, Cameron took off in the opposite direction at a fast gallop.

Drew and Rick joined the others to begin moving the herd toward Leaning Rock Crossing, and Drew wondered why the boss would want to hear about Chihara. What could he have in common with an Indian?

In his mind Drew could see a pudgy old man dressed in a white suit and riding in a two-horse-drawn carriage. He'd look a little like Colonel Walters. For a reason that surprised Drew, he was angry at the man. Why wasn't he out here helping them? He probably had enough money to buy every head of cattle in Arizona and Mexico. Since the cattle had calmed down, they plodded along at a steady pace, and Drew and Rick kept their places on the south side of the herd. The wind was from the south and there would be less dust.

It took at least an hour to reach Leaning Rock Crossing. The sun was still high in the sky, but since the cattle had exerted a lot of energy in the stampede, Cameron decided to have the drovers circle the herd early and finish the drive tomorrow.

"I guess that's how the place got its name," Rick said, breaking into Drew's thoughts. Glancing up and shielding his eyes from the sun's rays, Drew saw a granite pinnacle leaning precariously down toward the trail.

"That rock's been up there and leaning like that for thousands of years," Drew said, kneeing Nino Blanco ahead, "but it does put the hurry in your horse, doesn't it."

Rick laughed at him. It made him feel better to hear Drew joking for a change.

Not far from the crossing was a group of cottonwood trees by a clear-running stream. Drew saw a black stallion hobbled on the grassy bank and looked around for the white-suited fat man he'd imagined. But there was no carriage or two white horses.

Instead he saw a slender black-clad figure squatting

down by a fire where a large black stewpot bubbled away, giving off an aroma that set his mouth to watering. A movement by the stream caught his attention and he shifted his eyes in that direction. A brown-skinned boy was filling some canteens.

At the sound of the approaching riders, the slender figure by the pot stood up and looked around, at the same time pushing off a wide-brimmed black hat. Short curly red hair glistened in the light.

John Cameron rode toward the fire and dismounted. "Miss Wallace," he began, tipping his hat to the young woman who smiled up at him. "We had a stampede and these two fellows helped us. Drew Williams here"—he jerked his thumb over his shoulder toward Drew—"has a story that I think you will find very interesting."

Drew couldn't believe his ears or eyes. This couldn't be Jessie Wallace! The name implied a man. Maybe she was a daughter or a granddaughter. A woman that pretty couldn't be smart enough to be the boss of a cattle ranch. Dark brown and even brows framed green eyes. A straight nose above a full mouth gave her a defiant appearance.

As Drew dismounted, he watched her walk toward them with the grace of a cat.

"Miss Wallace," Cameron said, a slow smile beginning on his craggy face as if he'd known what Drew had been thinking about her, "this is Drew Williams and Rick Gregston."

Her smile was congenial but noncommittal. The interested look in her eyes was from mention of the stampede and had nothing to do with the two newcomers personally.

"Fellows," Cameron went on, the smile still there, "this is Jessie Wallace, owner of the Double J Ranch."

The trail boss pressed his mouth tightly shut so he wouldn't laugh at the shocked expression on both men's faces, especially Drew's.

"John said you had a story that would interest me," she said in a voice that was full of authority. "If it doesn't concern my cattle or ranch or that renegade Chihara, then don't waste my time." Inclining her head to one side she raised an eyebrow. There was a challenge in her eyes.

Drew was surprised at her brashness. Melissa has been brash at first, but that was just because she was spoiled. But something told Drew that this woman wasn't spoiled, just independent and hard working. He got the distinct feeling that he wouldn't want to be on Jessie Wallace's wrong side.

"Can't we talk while we eat?" Cameron asked, rubbing his stomach. "I'm as hungry as a hog with its mouth nailed shut." They all laughed as they tied their horses and crowded around the stewpot. The boy got tin plates from a box in a small wagon and passed them around.

"Why don't you fill your plate, then tell me what you know about Chihara?" Jessie Wallace suggested to Drew. She poured coffee into a tin cup and sat down on a flat rock. There was enough room on it for him to sit beside her.

The stew was a good change from the beans, bread, and jerky they'd eaten the past couple of days, and it was all Drew could do not to gobble it down.

"I know you must be hungry," she said pleasantly,

crossing her legs, "so why don't you just go ahead and eat, then tell me all about this." Narrowing her green eyes, she pulled her mouth into a bow then took a sip of coffee.

Drew nodded his thanks. He hadn't tasted anything this good in a long time. He shook his head when she asked if he wanted seconds. Taking his plate to the boy who handed him a steaming cup of coffee, Drew returned and sat down by the woman.

"Well," he began resolutely, swallowing a mouthful of coffee that was strong enough to hold up the leaning rock, "since your cattle are safe, I guess you want to know about Chihara, huh?"

"You're right," she said crisply, nodding slowly, batting her green eyes irritably.

"Why are you so interested in that Indian?" Drew asked. He was puzzled why a woman of her looks, age, and position would want to know about Indians instead of wanting to go to San Francisco or Denver and buy clothes. She turned an exasperated look up at him.

"I own the Double J Ranch, which begins on the other side of those rocks," she replied, brushing her hand impatiently over her short red hair. "I lose about ten head of cattle a year to that savage. It wouldn't be so bad if he'd come and ask for a few cows. But I guess he's too proud for that. He'd rather steal them." Anger tightened her slender face and her eyes snapped.

"Why don't you just ride over to his village and offer him the cows?" Drew's question was shrewd, and he looked at her with a lowered head and slight grin.

"You've got to be crazy!" Her voice exploded and her head snapped up. Her eyes widened in disbelief. "I wouldn't go across the border with anything less than an army patrol, and those aren't easy to come by."

She shook her head and dropped her gaze her black boots.

"Why is it so hard for the two of you to get together?" Drew asked, turning sideways on the rock to watch her. Jessie Wallace had a violence just under the surface of her femininity, and he knew it wouldn't take much to set her off.

"Because he's like all men," she answered in a soft, level tone. "No woman is smart enough to run a ranch—or anything else, for that matter—in a man's way of thinking. It would be beneath his dignity to have to ask a woman for help, and he certainly wouldn't take it if it was offered by a woman."

"And you're too stubborn to offer it." The thought turned into words and slipped out before Drew could stop them.

"I beg your pardon," she snapped, her eyes cold and her lips pressed tightly together. "Why are you in this part of the country, anyway?" Cocking an eyebrow she glared at him, waiting for an answer.

Once again, and feeling even more rehearsed, Drew recounted the past year and felt saddened when a sympathetic expression softened her eyes.

"I'm sorry," she said, lifting her hand. He thought she was going to touch him. Catching herself in time she dropped her hand to her lap. "What are you going to do when you catch up with Caleb Dayton?" she asked, turning her head sideways and chewing on the inside of her mouth.

"I'm going to kill him," Drew said simply in a cold voice, bitter and toneless. "He took away the best thing that ever happened to me, and there isn't a bad thing good enough for him. One of your riders saw him earlier and said that he was the one who started the stampede by firing a gun. He's also been giving guns to your friend Chihara."

Green hatred boiled in Drew again and he felt a knot form in his stomach.

"Where do you think he is now?" she asked, gripping her hands in her lap. Glancing down at them, Drew noticed that they were red, probably from going without gloves in the sun. They reminded him of Melissa on the trip to Tucson. He had to swallow before he could talk.

"Up ahead somewhere waiting for me and Rick, I would guess," he answered, shrugging his shoulders.

"Maybe this isn't the proper thing to say," she ventured, pressing her lips together, "but I think I'd rather be worried about that Indian and my cattle than being after Dayton with a vengeance. Why don't you let the sheriff or a marshal take care of it?" She sounded like Colonel Walters.

Drew looked at her for a long minute. He could understand the logic of her question, but it just didn't set well with him.

"I guess for the same reason you don't let someone run the ranch for you. You want to be sure the work gets done right." The reply sounded snide and sarcastic but that was the only way he could answer.

"Your point," she conceded, a soft smile tilting up the corners of her mouth. She relaxed against the rock and crossed her legs. She was a very pretty woman. But there was a hard side to her.

"How did you get to be the owner of a ranch?" Drew asked, forgetting the obvious. She was so young, though, and couldn't know that much about it.

As suddenly as the smile had softened her face, it disappeared and the stiffness returned. She sat up as rigid as a poker.

"Don't you think a woman is capable of owning and running a ranch?" she snapped. Hot anger flashed in her green eyes.

The loud sound of her voice turned John Cameron around from the stewpot where he was refilling his plate; he looked concerned. She shook her head at his raised brows.

"Miss Wallace," Drew said placidly, "there's no need to get upset. I was just wondering if you'd bought the ranch or had inherited it. I'd have asked the same thing if you'd been a man."

Drew knew he'd have done nothing of the sort, but that was another matter. Why make her angry? He'd only be there for a little while, anyway.

"I'm sorry," she said softly, standing up and looking down at him. "My father was killed three years ago in an Indian raid. No, it wasn't Chihara's people." The look on his face must have asked the question. "They were a bunch of Indians north of here. Since then, John Cameron, Bush Waggoner, and I have kept the place going. I'm very proud of it."

The sparkling look in her eyes said as much as did the tone in her voice. Rick came wandering over to them, a plate of stew in his hand.

"Are we going to ride on tonight?" he asked Drew, chewing on a good-sized piece of meat. Before Drew could answer, she did.

"Since it's so late," she began, looking down at the ground, a pink hue coloring her fair face, "Why don't you two come by the ranch, replenish your grub sacks, and get an early start tomorrow? Maybe then your limp will be better."

Cameron, a sly smile on his face, joined them. He'd heard the last part of what she'd said.

"She's right," he agreed, pushing back his hat. "One more day won't make any difference. You can get killed tomorrow same as you can today. Nobody's going to care if you die like a fool going after that old man instead of letting the law do its job."

Drew didn't mind giving in too much. He was curious to see how a ranch that was run by a woman would look. In fact, he was so wrapped up in that thought that he didn't take offense at Cameron's last remark.

"I guess you're right," he said, looking self-consciously from Rick to Jessie, to Cameron, and back to Rick.

The drovers had finally gotten the cattle bedded down for the night and were coming in to eat. After they'd eaten their fill, the young boy gathered up the plates, cups, and forks, put them with the sand-cleaned stewpot and coffeepot in a box and carried it over to a small two-wheeled cart. Coming back he kicked sand over the fire, untied the burro, and hitched it to the cart. Nodding and smiling at Jessie Wallace, he climbed up into the cart and started riding northwest.

The rest mounted up and followed. Drew was only mildly aware of the easy way Jessie Wallace mounted the black stallion and rode like a seasoned rider.

It took an hour to reach the sprawling ranch. The sun was still high enough in the blue sky for Drew to see some of it. The white adobe and red-cobblestone-roofed house was something Drew wasn't prepared for. He'd expected a rundown frame house with grass growing wild in the yard. But that wasn't so.

Multicolored flowers hung in baskets along the bare-raftered porch. Black wrought-iron tables and chairs with bright-colored cushions looked comfortable, and desert flowers and cactus grew around the house.

"This wasn't what you expected, is it?" Jessie asked, a smirk pulling her mouth to one side. Her brows were arched.

"No," he answered truthfully, shaking his head slowly. He drew the word out, feeling his face turn red. "Not exactly. It's very nice. I can see why you're proud of it. Melissa would have loved a place like it."

He spoke the words before he was aware of them. Pain as though from a hot knife shot through him. He wished he hadn't let his guard down. He'd been doing so well until then.

"The bunkhouse is this way," Cameron said, reaching out and touching Drew's arm, a sad look in his eyes.

Drew shook his head quickly to clear away the painful thoughts, and he and Rick reined their horses around to follow Cameron.

The long bunkhouse was about two hundred yards from the main house, and the lively sounds of a harmonica drifted from the open window. A wrangler came, took the reins of the three horses, and led them toward the corral.

Drew limped inside and sat down on a bunk that appeared to belong to no one. He bent over and began rubbing his aching knee.

"Hurts pretty bad, huh?" Cameron asked. When Drew nodded, he went into the kitchen and returned with a bottle of brown liniment. Drew rolled up his pants leg, poured some of the foul-smelling liquid into his hands, and rubbed it on his knee. It had already swollen and turned black and blue.

"That should make it better by morning," Drew said, curling up his sore lip at the awful odor, "or it will be rotted all the way through." Removing his hat, Drew stretched out on the bunk, then bent his knee because it hurt too much to straighten it. Rick and Cameron laughed at him. Rick turned and walked away.

"Do you want to talk for a minute?" Cameron asked, looking down at Drew.

"Sure," Drew replied, doubling up a pillow and stuffing it under his head. He wasn't sleepy; just bone-tired. "What do you want to talk about? Cattle? Miss Wallace? The Indian?"

Each time Cameron shook his head, his eyes narrowing. Going to the table, he got a chair and returned to the bunk.

"You said you were going to kill this Dayton fellow when you find him," Cameron began, a shine beginning in his eyes. "How are you going to do it? Rope? Gun? Knife?"

Letting his thoughts run wild for a second, Drew

was quiet. Then he shook his head with a jerk.

"In view of what Dayton has done to me," Drew finally said in a whisper, "I've thought of several ways. Everything from staking him to an anthill and pouring sugar on him to tying scorpions on him." He shivered at the thoughts again.

"I've got a way I'll bet you haven't thought of." Cameron's eyes gleamed, and he was breathing harshly through flared nostrils.

"What?" Drew asked slowly, coming up on his right elbow. There was something wild about Cameron's eyes. They had a glazed expression.

"I heard that some drovers over in Texas caught two rustlers," Cameron began, nodding slowly and hitching the chair closer. His eyes narrowed. "The thing they did to him wasn't very pretty." His breathing became sharper.

"What thing?" Drew asked impatiently, wanting to choke him.

"You know how rawhide shrinks in the sun." It was more of a statement than a question. Drew nodded slowly.

"The drovers took the hides of the two cows that had been killed, tied the rustlers up inside, and left them out in the hot sun all day." The last two words slipped over Cameron's tongue like slow water over pebbles. Cameron leaned forward in the chair, his eyes wide and shining.

Drew closed his eyes as the image of two men tied inside a green hide took form in his mind. He could almost hear them screaming as the hide began tightening around them and slowly squeezing their ribs against their lungs, shutting off the air.

Cameron was right. That was one way he'd never thought of. It was a good way.

Cameron flopped back in the chair, slapped his hands down against his thigh, and roared in laughter.

"Don't you think that would be a perfect way for Dayton to die for what he did to your wife?" Cameron asked, coughing and clearing his throat. He nodded and narrowed his eyes.

"Well, it would get the job done," Drew agreed, turning his head sideways and watching Cameron skeptically. "But I hadn't planned to spend that much time on him. I'd thought about just shooting him and getting it over and done with."

"No," Cameron argued, shaking his head rapidly and frowning. "That's not good enough. I think you ought to do it this way."

Drew couldn't understand Cameron's attitude. Why was he getting such pleasure out of this diabolical method of killing someone?

"I'll give it some thought," Drew replied with a half-smile, lying back on the pillow and closing his eyes. In a little while he heard the chair being replaced at the table and then the door closed.

The liniment helped ease the pain in his knee some, and soon sleep worked its magic in restoring strength to his body.

Chapter VII

A hand shaking Drew's shoulder awoke him from a deep sleep. The afternoon shadows were creeping across the floor as the sun slid down in the sky. Bush Waggoner was bending over him, a wide smile on his bearded face.

"What do you want?" Drew asked thickly, squinting to see who it was in the dim light.

"Oh, and it's not what I be wantin'," Waggoner replied in the strange brogue, arching his bushy brows. "It's Miss Wallace that wants to be seein' ye."

What in the world could she want? Drew wondered irritably, swinging his legs over the side of the bunk. His left knee had stiffened a little, but a couple of kicks took it away. The smelly liniment had worked.

Running his fingers through his hair, he put his hat on and followed Waggoner toward the house. The sweet scent of flowers drifted across the yard on the warm breeze. The weather was pleasant and a bird sang in a nearby cactus.

A figure sat in one of the wrought-iron chairs, and

once again Drew's mind played tricks on him. Although this wasn't the part of the country where he'd wanted to settle, it was easy to imagine that it was Melissa sitting there waiting for him.

But reality struck him when he stepped up on the low rock porch. Jessie Wallace had changed from her black riding clothes to a short-sleeved, round-neck lavender dress with a simple straight skirt that came just to the tops of her bare feet. Doing a doubletake, Drew still couldn't believe his eyes. It was unthinkable for a woman to let her feet be seen. No respectable woman would do such a thing.

"What's the matter, Mr. Williams?" she asked, mischief in her green eyes. Her brows arched and a smirking grin pulled at the corners of her mouth. "Haven't you ever seen a woman's bare feet?"

He could feel the blood rush up to his face at her perception. "Yes, of course," he muttered, "but . . ." Her laughter filled the air.

"But not on someone who's supposed to be a refined lady, is that it?" Catching her underlip between strong white teeth she watched him. He was shocked at her self-assessment.

"Well, it's not that, so much," he replied, swallowing hard. "It's just that in this part of the country there are so many things that could bite you. Crawly things, you know."

She held his gaze for a long time, then raked her eyes up and down his tall and lean frame. He felt almost naked.

"Do you bite, Mr. Williams?" The question apparently didn't bother her any, but it almost knocked Drew out of his boots! Even Sara Judson, daughter of Tucson's sheriff, hadn't been this bold! Bush Waggoner roared in laughter, turned, and walked away, shaking his head all the time.

"Only when I see something worth biting," he replied drolly, wondering what kind of game she was playing with him. "Miss Wallace, let's stop this nonsense. Why did you want to see me?"

"Sit down, Mr. Williams," she offered, inclining her head toward the other chair on the opposite side of the table. "Would you like some lemonade?" He shook his head and she went on: "Something stronger?" Her face was set and stern now. All the joking was done.

"Bourbon, if you have it," he replied, sitting down on the red cushion. She called out, and it wasn't long before the young boy appeared carrying a tray with a bottle of amber-colored liquid and two glasses.

Reaching out her sunburned hands she poured a liberal portion into each glass and passed one over to him. Drew had another shock coming when she picked up her glass and downed a healthy swallow. He had the idea that she was just showing off for him and that she'd cough her head off, struggle for breath, and turn red. But she swallowed easily, as if she'd been doing it for a long time. He knew he was staring at her again.

"What's the matter now, Mr. Williams?" she asked placidly, real puzzlement drawing her brows together. "Don't tell me that you've never seen a lady drink bourbon?" She squinted her eyes in a challenge.

"Well, I've seen women drink bourbon," Drew answered dryly, taking a sip of the best bourbon he'd tasted in a long time. "But they weren't ladies, they didn't own ranches, and they didn't talk the way you do." He was rambling and couldn't seem to stop.

The stiffness went out of her body and she relaxed back against the chair. She threw back her head as clear and genuine laughter burst out and rang across the porch.

"Mr. Williams," she said, clearing her throat and shaking her head, "you amaze me. I graduated from a finishing school in New York three years ago. I learned to dance properly, which fork to use, and how to hold a teacup. That wasn't for me. All prissy and proper. I had to wear shoes all the time. I came home, learned to ride a horse, build a campfire, brand a cow, and run a ranch. I know all about cattle, droughts, and floods. When Dad was killed I knew what to do."

So she wasn't some spoiled rich girl, he told himself, taking another sip. She had a right to have a hard side.

"Miss Wallace," he said slowly, stretching his left leg out to ease the stiffness, "you didn't send for me just to talk about your education or how well you can run a ranch. What's really on your mind?"

Putting the glass down, she crossed her legs, smoothed the cloth over her knees, and wiggled her toes. Leaning back in the chair she looked him straight in the eye for a time.

"I want you to bring Chihara here." Her voice and eyes were steady and calm. She would probably have looked and sounded the same if she'd asked him for the time of day.

Drew wouldn't have been any more shocked if she'd asked him to walk barefoot through a bull-nettle patch.

"You want me to do what?" Drew asked, the glass midway to his mouth. He knew he was really staring at her this time and that his mouth was hanging open. He closed his eyes and shook his head.

"I want you to bring Chihara here," she repeated as simply as before. Her expression didn't change.

"Chihara?" he repeated, leaning forward and frowning. "Why do you want him brought here? Why me?"

Drew had no intention of going back across the border to get that crazy Indian, but he was eaten up with curiosity. He had to know why a woman of her standing would want to see him.

"I've been giving some thought to what you said about letting the Indians have enough meat to do them for a whole year," she replied, shrugging her shoulders. "That would probably be less than what they steal from me. The reason I want you to go is that you've actually been in the camp and would know how to get back there. You could probably handle him."

Reaching up and touching his broken nose, Drew threw back his head and roared in laughter. His back still ached.

"Miss Wallace," he said contritely, "does this look like I know how to handle that man? I can hardly breathe because of one of his well-placed kicks in the back. Besides, he knows I'm after Dayton—and Dayton's been giving him guns for a long time. You'd probably have better luck with him. Why don't you, Waggoner, and Cameron go see him?"

A look brightened in her eyes and he knew what

she was planning.

"Oh, no," he said, shaking his head rapidly, "I won't go with you."

The expression still didn't change on her smooth face. Her green eyes still had an amused gleam.

"But you managed to escape," she insisted, lowering her head and still holding his gaze.

There was nothing that would get Drew to tell her that a small girl had helped him and Rick escape, or that the escape had been made easier because Chihara was drunk. What she didn't know couldn't make a fool out of him. That had happened too often.

"Miss Wallace," Drew said slowly, standing up and hooking his thumbs over his belt, "that Indian almost killed me and Rick. I don't see any reason to give him another chance."

She frowned deeply, the color in her eyes deepening in anger at being defied.

"Mr. Williams," she said crisply, pressing her lips together tightly, "you don't strike me as being the cowardly type. I thought you'd jump at the chance to go back and make him pay for what he did to you and your cousin."

Drew threw back his head and laughed again. "Lady," he said, arching his brows, "there's a difference between being a coward and being cautious. If I went back to Chihara's camp to make him pay for what he did to me and Rick, there wouldn't be enough of him to bring back!"

Snapping her head up, she stared at Drew, then blinked her eyes rapidly.

"You don't appear to be a violent man either," she said, folding her hands in her lap.

"I'm not," he answered, walking to the edge of the porch. "But I try to take care of me and mine. The time I took going back after Chihara could be used in going after Dayton."

Drawing her lips against her teeth she shook her head. "You're one stubborn man, Drew Williams." She paused for a second. "But I'll tell you what. After you finish your business with whoever, come back to the Double J. Work for me and I'll make it worth your while."

Her voice was as serious as the look in her eyes, and Drew knew she meant a job, nothing more. Or did he see something in the back of her eyes?

"You could have a deal," he said, nodding and smiling down at her. Drew was surprised and touched when she stood up, rose on tiptoe, and kissed him softly on his unshaven cheek. Without saying anything, he turned and started for the bunkhouse.

The sun had disappeared down behind the mountains, and deep shadows were long across the yard. A cool breeze drifted across the wasteland.

Drew was stepping up on the end of the bunkhouse porch when a long burly arm reached out, grabbed him around the neck, and jerked him around the corner of the building.

"I don't know who you are, mister, or what you're doing here." The voice was gruff and strong in Drew's ear. Judging from the position of the man's right arm, Drew guessed he was about his height or a little taller. "But I'm warning you: Stay away from Miss Wallace! She belongs to me! Do you understand?"

Having no choice, Drew nodded. The assailant switched arms and hit Drew as hard as he could over the right kidney. Drew doubled over as the wind was knocked out of him.

Quickly drawing in his breath, Drew had a surprise for the man. Straightening up he spun around and lashed out with his right fist, catching the man squarely on the jaw. Then, bringing up his right knee, he planted it sharply in the man's groin. Howling in pain, the man dropped to his knees and doubled over, holding the injured part of his body.

Thinking that enough unjust pain and injury had been inflicted on his body in the past few days, Drew thought it was time that someone else suffered a little also.

As the man looked up at him, the former army scout lifted his moccasined foot and kicked him under the chin as hard as he could. Blood spewed from the man's mouth when his teeth cut into his tongue. The man fell back on the ground like a wet rag and moaned. He sounded like he was dying. Drew knew he wasn't, but wouldn't have really cared if he actually were.

Everyone on this ranch, with the possible exception of Bush Waggoner, was crazy! That was the only explanation. Cameron had a nasty idea in how to kill Dayton, Jessie Wallace wanted him to go after an Indian who'd tried to kick him to death, and now this man was accusing him of something he'd given no thought to.

"Now, let me tell you something," Drew said coldly and slowly, bending down so the man could hear him over his own groaning. "Miss Wallace and I were discussing a job. Nothing more. She's a beautiful woman, but I don't have any room for her or any other woman in my life right now."

The man struggled to his feet, holding the front part of his pants with one hand and wiping away the blood with the other. In the dim light Drew could see the man's face. He needed a shave, and with the blood on the stubble he looked like he'd been in a war.

"But I saw her kissing you," he whined, his mutilated, bleeding tongue sticking out.

"My God, man," Drew said, shaking his head and wanting to laugh, "she would just as soon have kissed a puppy."

Drew stepped back and watched the man pull himself together. "Now I'm going to the bunkhouse and get some rest, so Rick and I can leave tomorrow to go after a man who killed my wife and child last week."

If he'd waited, Drew would have seen a shocked frown on the man's swelling face. Turning on his heel Drew stomped up on the porch, opened the door, went over to the bunk, and dropped down. The aches in his knee, arm, and now his back were catching up with him again, and he wondered seriously if he'd live long enough to catch up with Dayton—or even through the night, for that matter.

Riders came in, others went out. Those who came in, took off their boots and gunbelts, stretched out on the bunks, and soon various snorts, squeaks, and snores filled the long and narrow room.

Drew was about to doze off when a hand shook his shoulder. Opening his eyes slowly, Drew wasn't actually surprised to see John Cameron bending over him in the deepening shadows.

"What can I do for you, Cameron?" Drew asked dully, taking a deep breath and wishing he'd never gotten involved with this crazy man. He and Rick should have kept on riding when they first heard the stampeding cattle.

"Well," Cameron said enthusiastically, taking Drew's question as interest. "After I met you I began doing some thinking. I've been working here for a long time. Up early every morning. Late to bed. Cattle, snakes, and not enough rain. What you're doing in going after the Dayton fellow sounds better to me. Why don't I just ride along with you and your cousin? I could be a big help." He bent closer to see Drew better in the dimness.

Immediately Drew was reminded of the time when Tag Cooper had wanted to go along with him for adventure when he was going after Slade Dayton. But this was more than he could handle. This was a grown man. Not some kid!

"No, I don't think so," Drew replied, expelling the breath and shaking his head on the pillow. "I don't want to be responsible for anyone other than Rick and me."

Cameron was quiet for a time but Drew could still feel him standing by the bunk.

"What time are you going to leave in the morning?" Cameron asked, a strange tone in his voice.

"Oh, around daybreak, I guess. Why?" Drew guessed that Cameron was thinking he was going to ride along with them whether they wanted him to or not.

Suddenly a thought took shape in Drew's tired mind. He was through with being encumbered with other people slowing him down and throwing hindrances in his catching up with Dayton.

"Oh, nothing," Cameron answered glibly. "I was just thinking about how much has happened since yesterday. If you're sure you don't need me to go along with you, I'll try to see you before you leave." Turning on his heel, Cameron clomped across the wooden floor, opened the door, and slammed it closed behind him.

Drew lay still for a second to be sure Cameron was gone. Raising up on his elbow he looked down the long row of bunks. He could see Rick's long legs hanging over the side.

"Rick," he started to call out, but stopped. Getting up, he eased down between the bunks until he reached his cousin. Bending down, he shook Rick's shoulder and immediately the sleeping man awoke.

"What's wrong?" Rick mumbled, blinking his eyes slowly and pushing back his hair.

"If we want to save ourselves a lot of trouble," Drew said, squatting down by the bunk so he wouldn't have to talk so loud, "we'll leave the Double J Ranch as soon as we can get our gear together."

"What kind of trouble?" Rick asked, leaning closer to see Drew and frowning. "Why will we be in trouble if we stay here?"

"Not if we stay here," Drew whispered. "Cameron wants to go with us after Dayton in the morning."

"Oh, God, no," Rick protested vehemently and in disbelief, shaking his head rapidly. "That man needs a few cards for a full deck." He swung his legs over the side of the bunk and sat up.

"I know," Drew agreed, standing up. "Go to the

corral and saddle our horses. We're going to leave as soon as we can tonight. I'm going to the cookhouse and get a grub sack together. If Cameron sees either of us, maybe he'll think we're just getting things ready early for tomorrow."

Rick pulled on his boots and stood up. Pushing his hair back again, he jammed his hat down.

"Will you be sure and tell me what brought all this on?" Rick asked as they walked toward the door. "I'd have thought you'd want to spend a couple of days here and, ah, rest. From the way you and Miss Wallace were talking today, anybody could see she had her eye on you. She don't look too bad, you know." He raised his brows suggestively.

Drew couldn't suppress the laugh that escaped. "Whoa," he said, swatting Rick across the shoulder. "She or any other woman is the last thing I need right now. But let's get out of here while we can, before Cameron decides on some other way to help us."

Before Rick could ask any more questions, Drew started out toward the cookhouse at a trot. That was the fastest movement his knee would allow. When all of this was over, he promised himself, he'd treat himself to a week of resting and eating at the finest restaurant in the first big town he came to.

The cook didn't ask any questions when Drew told him he wanted a grub sack. Apparently he was used to riders coming in and asking for such on short notice.

"Would you have any peaches?" Drew asked, starting to pull the drawstring together. "Dried would be all right."

"Sure," the cook said, throwing Drew a strange

look and shrugging his shoulders. He went to the storeroom and returned with a paper sack. "These are dried and should last a few days."

"Thanks," Drew said, putting the sack in with the rest and pulling the string tight. Rick was waiting at the steps with both horses when Drew came out.

"Let's go before Cameron sees us," Drew said, looping the grub sack over the saddle horn and swinging up. They had to ride past the house to head north, and a motion from the front window caught Drew's eye.

A hotel window in Tucson flashed in his mind. He could see a figure standing in the shadows. But this wasn't Tucson and that wasn't a hotel. Did Jessie Wallace just happen to be looking out the window or had she suspected that they might leave early? No, she was just standing there. How could she know, when he'd only decided to leave a few minutes ago himself?

The night was warm but not hot, and the horses were rested and fed. "Let 'um go," Drew said, expelling a long breath. The sharp kick in the white horse's side exploded his energy and the long legs stretched out. Rick did the same thing to Money Man, and it wasn't long before the lights of the Double J were lost behind hills and gullies.

The moonlight washed the land with a coat of silver and it was easy for the men to find their way.

"Do you get the feeling that we've just escaped from a crazy house?" Drew asked Rick over his shoulder as they rode along.

"Well, I've been in more pleasant places," Rick answered with a snort, riding up by him.

Cold fingers ran up and down Drew's back. He felt as if a hundred eyes were watching them. Past experience told him that Caleb Dayton was probably on top of one of those hills and laughing at him. A premonition told him that if he and Rick slept outside tonight they wouldn't wake to see tomorrow.

"Rick, something tells me that we'd better find some kind of shelter for the rest of the night." Dread and apprehension edged his voice.

"Why? What's the matter?" Rick asked, with a tone in his voice that let Drew know he was as scared as he was.

"Dayton is just too close," Drew answered, trying to swallow the dry lump in his throat. "As tired as we both are, if we're sleeping out in the open, he could slip up on us and we'd never know it."

Defeat and weariness replaced the apprehension in Drew's voice. Suddenly he felt tired in every bone in his body.

The good Lord and luck were on their side. Topping a hill, they were astonished and relieved to see an abandoned adobe hut at the bottom of the draw about a hundred yards away. A cobble roof and stone porch ran the length of the hut.

"That's a sight for sore eyes," Drew almost shouted in disbelief. Reaching the hut they tied the horses to an oak tree, unsaddled them, and carried the gear inside. The hut had only one room, and for now the moonlight lit up the whole place.

"What did you mean about a crazy house?" Rick asked, kicking out his bedroll. Drew could see a frown on his cousin's face, but couldn't tell what it meant. "Why were you in such a big hurry to leave the

Double J anyway? Was it John Cameron or Jessie Wallace?" The frown turned to a grin.

"Both, I guess," Drew answered truthfully, flopping down on the bedroll. He squinted his eyes in the semidarkness. "They wanted me to do things for them and with them that I didn't have the time or stomach for."

Rick had stretched out on his blanket and against the saddle, his arms under his head, but he jerked up at the disgusted tone in Drew's voice.

"Just what in the devil did Jessie Wallace want you to do for or with her that you couldn't stomach?" There was a jibe in Rick's voice and a gleam in his eyes. "It couldn't have been that bad."

Drew burst out in ribald laughter when the meaning of Rick's words hit him.

"No," he said, clearing his throat. "Too bad it couldn't have been something like that. She wanted me to go back to the Yaqui camp and bring Chihara to her."

Rick's mouth dropped open and his eyes bulged in their sockets. "What?" he exploded, his brows wrinkling. "She has to be crazy. That Indian would kill you on sight! Why would she want you to do a dumb thing like that? Was John Cameron's request as stupid?"

When Drew finished describing Cameron's fate for Dayton with a raw cowhide, Rick grimaced, shuddered his shoulders, and then burst out laughing.

"Now, that makes a lot of sense to me," Rick said, stretching out again on his blanket. "What do you think?"

For a long time Drew didn't answer. He stared out

the window. "No," he finally said, shaking his head slowly. "It wouldn't be right to kill an animal just so we could watch the breath slowly being squeezed out of Caleb Dayton. It would serve him right, though."

Like a jack-in-the-box Rick snapped up again, and he leaned closer to see Drew better.

"Why not?" he asked shortly. Anger hardened his voice. "What in the Sam Hill's wrong with you? Dayton didn't give a hoot in Hades about what was right and wrong when he slit Melissa's throat and shot her in the stomach. He could tell in one glance that she was pregnant, and he didn't give a second thought about killing your little girl. So don't sit there and talk to me about what's right and wrong!"

Drew had seen Rick when he was happy and when he was angry and when he was scared half to death. But he'd never thought he'd hear him this brutal with words. Apparently he'd missed what Drew had said and meant.

"What are you getting so mad about?" Drew asked harshly. "Dayton is going to get what's coming to him." Cold certainty edged his words. "But like I just said, I'm not going to kill an animal in order to kill an animal." Pausing for a breath Drew gritted his teeth. "That's all Dayton can be called—a mad animal! Unless something happens to the contrary, I want it to be face to face with Dayton. I want to look him straight in the eye. I want him to know exactly why he's going to die." Then a thought struck him. "I want you to promise to do me a favor."

Rick was silent for a minute. Then he cleared his throat. "I know what you're thinking and are going to ask," he finally said. "But you don't have to. If luck happened to get on his side, I'll blow his brains out!"

There was enough venom in Rick's voice to kill the meanest rattlesnake in the desert.

"We'd better try and get some sleep while the getting is good," Drew suggested, turning on his side and pulling his hat down over his eyes. Sleep should come soon: he was bone-tired. His shoulder hurt and a nagging ache throbbed in his knee. But why should tonight be any different? It wouldn't be the first sleepless night he'd gone through since Melissa had been killed.

Bending his knee didn't help the ache, so he turned over on his back and stretched his leg out. But that didn't help either. Keeping his leg straight he rose to a squatting position and stood up. Glancing at Rick, Drew could tell from his cousin's deep breathing that he was already fast asleep. That was the advantage of being clean-minded.

Drew tiptoed and limped across the stone floor over to the window, pushed it open, and leaned his arms on the sill. Somewhere out there, probably watching the hut at that very minute, was an old man who'd turned Drew's life into a living hell in only a few days. Drew realized that until he caught up with Dayton, there would be little sleep or rest for him. His life had been wrecked, and he couldn't begin to put it back together until Dayton was dead!

Easing across the floor Drew stepped out into the warm night air. The moon slid behind a cloud, and for a minute everything was thrown into darkness. Just as the moon appeared again, a coyote's lonely cry echoed from a hill.

Another sound rustled in the grassy arroyo at the

side of the hut. It was louder than the coyotes. Drawing the Colt .45, Drew moved quietly across the porch. He knew it was Dayton. No other thought entered his mind. He could see the tall thin man with the flopped-down hat squatting in the weeds just waiting for him to get close enough to drop him with the buffalo gun.

But this time he wasn't going to give Dayton the chance to ride away again and laugh at him.

He wished he'd brought the rifle, but he was close enough to Dayton that the .45 would do the job. The rustling sound suddenly stopped. Had Dayton seen him? Drew's mouth was dry. His hands were wet.

Dayton probably thinks he's enticed me close enough, Drew told himself, a sardonic smile on his thin lips. Squatting down he inched forward in short steps. His knee ached, but soon the whole thing would be over and he could rest his whole body. Dayton would be dead, Melissa's murderer would be punished, and he could begin putting his life back together again.

The moon came out from behind a cloud and everything around him was as plain as day. Drew could see Dayton clearly now. He had his back to him and his face was obscured in the shadows.

"Dayton, you murdering bastard, I've got you now," Drew shouted, jumping up. Holding the .45 in both hands and aiming at the dark figure, Drew pulled the trigger. The sound echoed down the canyon as yellow flame burst from the pistol. Once again Drew pulled the trigger. Again and again and again. He pulled the trigger once more, and kept pulling it even when it landed on an empty cartridge.

"Drew, what in the name of God are you doing?" Rick's shocked voice and his hands shaking Drew's shoulders penetrated the haze that clouded Drew's mind. The acrid smell of gunpowder hung in the air. Drew brushed his hand across his eyes and shook his head.

"I just put six bullets in Caleb Dayton." Satisfaction edged his voice and he took a deep breath. He smiled at Rick and nodded.

"Dayton?" Rick questioned doubtfully, looking down at the ground and then back at Drew. "Where is he? I don't see anyone."

"Right there," Drew replied crossly, pointing to a spot on the ground. How could Rick be so blind? The old hider's body was right there in plain sight. Anyone could see it all huddled up.

"That's not a body," Rick said sorrowfully, coming back from where Drew had pointed. "You only put six bullets in the stump of a dead tree." Pity softened his voice. Drew had finally gone off the deep end, just as he had suspected he would.

"You're lying to me," Drew accused loudly through clenched teeth. "Dayton was waiting for me to come out here. He couldn't get us in the cabin. He made noises to get me to come outside. He's there. He's dead. I know he is."

Drew was breathing hard. His lungs felt as if they were on fire and his mouth was still dry. It hadn't tasted like this since he and Tag Cooper had gone to the canyon after Slade Dayton.

"No, Drew," Rick insisted patiently. Walking slowly toward him, Rick reached out and took the pistol from Drew's hand, which was hanging limply at his side. "Dayton isn't dead. Believe me. That's only a tree stump. Look closer. Come on, I'll go with you."

Taking Drew by the arm, Rick gently led him closer to the dark shape on the ground. Drew had to blink his eyes several times before his brain would accept the fact that Rick was right. As his thinking cleared he could recognize the riddled mess of splinters that was indeed a stump. Dayton would never know it, but he'd made a fool out of Drew once more.

All of Drew's will power slowly ebbed away, and the blood in his body turned cold while his knees buckled under him. The bright light of the moon slowly turned into darkness as his eyes closed. He never knew when he hit the ground. Rick tried to catch him, but Drew's sudden movement caught him off guard and he could only ease the fall a little.

Bright sunlight poured through the window. Its rays were warm, almost hot, on Drew's face. Blinking his eyes a couple of times, he moved his head out of the brightness and looked around the hut.

Rick was sitting on a short stool in the corner holding a cup of steaming coffee between his hands. His face was drawn and his eyes were tired.

"Welcome back to the land of the living," Rick said, a gentle smile and soft expression in his eyes. "Do you want some coffee?"

Drew wondered why he sounded so patronizing. "Yeah," he answered, pulling himself into a sitting position. "It smells good." A dull ache in his head slowed his movement a little.

While Rick poured the coffee and was bringing it

to him, Drew pushed back his hair and ran a hand over his face. He was puzzled at the stubble of beard he felt. That was strange. He'd only shaved yesterday. His eyes asked the silent question as he looked up at Rick to take the tin coffee cup from him.

"Two days," Rick replied, arching his brows and pulling his mouth to one side. "You've been asleep two days. I think your snoring put several new holes in the walls."

A small grin was all that Rick got for his joke but it didn't bother him. At least Drew was awake instead of thrashing around on the floor, mumbling wild things about the Daytons and calling sadly for Melissa. He doubted if the sleep had done Drew any good.

"You're probably as hungry as a bear," Rick surmised, turning back around to the oval oven built in the wall. "I saved some bread and meat for you."

He understood the bewilderment in Drew's eyes but decided to wait and let him make the first statement.

"I made a fool out of myself, didn't I?" Drew said more than asked. He drained the cup.

Rick had never seen a more dejected human being in all of his life. "No more than I would have under the circumstances," he reflected sympathetically. "You hadn't slept in days. You'd been kicked, beaten, had been cut on your arm, and a danged horse nearly fell on you. It's a wonder you held together as good as you did."

He handed Drew a tin plate with meat, beans, and a wedge of hot bread on it. There was even a small fried peach pie on the plate.

"If we don't find Dayton soon," Drew said softly,

splitting open the bread and putting the meat between it, "I'm going to lose my mind."

He almost choked when he tried to swallow a bite. A gulp of coffee washed it down. He started to put the plate aside but Rick wouldn't let him.

"Look, Drew, you haven't eaten in two days," Rick's voice was scolding. He refilled his cup and pulled the stool closer to Drew. "The food might not do your thinking any good, but it will put some grit in your bones. Now eat all of that or I'm going to feed it to you."

The sternness in Rick's voice snapped Drew's head up, and he smiled a little at the gleam in Rick's eyes. He knew that Rick was right. If he was to keep on after Dayton, he would have to get his mind straight and put some strength back into his body.

He did feel a smattering better after he'd eaten the sandwich and pie. The warmth of the coffee coursed through his body and the cold feeling began ebbing away. He couldn't understand why he was so cold. The sun was shining brightly and it was actually hot in the hut. Taking a deep breath, the stench of his own sweat and body odor made his nose wrinkle and his lips curl.

"I think I need a bath," he said, looking sheepishly up at Rick. "Did you happen to find any water around here? Surely you didn't just sit in here with me all the time while I was asleep."

Rick threw back his head and laughed. "No," he answered, still smiling. "You needed sleep, not someone to hold your hand. There's a little pond in back of the hut. I agree. You do need to wash behind your ears."

Taking clean clothes and soap from the saddlebag, Drew limped out behind the hut and found the pond. It was about twenty feet across and not quite six feet deep, as it only came up to his armpits when he undressed and waded out to the middle of it.

He lathered all over, then squatted completely under the water. Standing up, he squeezed the water out of his hair and eyes. He felt a hundred percent better after he'd dressed and shaved.

Curiosity got hold of him and he went to the opposite side of the hut. It didn't take much looking to find the stump that he'd massacred two days ago. In disbelief he looked down at what he'd done with six shells. If the stump hadn't been as large as it was, several of the bullets would have missed completely. No two bullets were close in the splintered mess. He couldn't believe that he'd let his tired mind play such a silly trick on him. For a short while it was funny and he smiled. But the smile faded and the driving, hot rage consumed him again.

Spinning around on his heel, Drew stomped through the weeds back to the hut. Rick was sitting on the porch in a chair tilted back against the wall. His hat was pulled low over his eyes and he was chewing on a blade of grass.

"We've wa—*I've* caused us to waste enough time," Drew said, going into the hut. He stuffed his dirty clothes into the saddlebag. Jerking the bedroll together, he hurried outside, swung the blanket and saddle on Nino Blanco, and climbed up.

Apparently Rick had anticipated what Drew would do, because he already had his bedroll tied up, and in a matter of minutes they were on their way north.

Hot rage and burning vengeance was the main reason Drew kicked the white horse in the side, and in no time at all a lot of ground had been covered between them and Caleb Dayton.

Chapter VIII

The trail that Drew and Rick had been following so relentlessly for some twenty miles from Mexico finally ended here. Carmen was a small sleepy town in Arizona circled on three sides by green mountains and open to the desert on the south. The bright noonday sun beat down on the two men as they rode into town. The dusty street was filled with people, horses, and wagons. The tracks they had been following were lost in the jumble of the others. A shaggy black dog nipped at the horses' heels and they skittered nervously to get away from the annoying mongrel.

"Do you think he's here?" Rick asked, pulling on the reins to calm Money Man.

"Yes," Drew replied, nodding slowly, his eyes snapping. His heart slammed against his ribs. "If the tracks that we've been following the past day and a half are his, Dayton is here. That same chip is in the tracks we've been following. We only lost the tracks as we came into town."

He took a deep breath and his shoulders slumped. Then he straightened up in the saddle. Pressing his mouth against his teeth, Drew jerked his hat off and took a swat at the dog. That did the trick. Tucking its tail between its legs, the dog beat a hasty retreat, and, whining now, ran under the porch of the mercantile store.

"You just saved that mutt's life," Rick said, an aggravated knot working in his jaw. "I was going to shoot him."

"Ah, he was just showing off," Drew replied, a small smile on his mouth. "You know," he continued, looking sideways at Rick, a gleam in his eyes that hadn't been there for a long time, "we haven't had a good beer in a week. I could sure use one right now. Couldn't you? That stuff in Mexico wasn't fit to wash your feet in. How about it? I'll buy."

Rick frowned at him, and Drew knew instantly what had caused it. How could he be thinking of Dayton one second and a beer the next?

"If Dayton's here," he went on, "we'll find him. If he's not, we'll ride on with a good taste in our mouth. Besides, where else but a saloon is the best place to ask questions?"

"You're right," Rick agreed, a smile replacing the frown. He smacked his lips.

The Full Glass saloon was halfway down the street between the bank and dry-goods store. There were several horses tied at the hitch rack. But no mule. Dismounting, Drew looked up and down the street. A pair of mules were hitched to a wagon in front of the dry-goods store, but no single mule.

Tying their horses to the hitch rail they shouldered their way through the well-oiled batwings. The smells of whiskey, beer, and smoke filled the air. The Full Glass wasn't very full, so there was plenty of room at the long polished bar. A shiny brass rail at the bottom ran the full length of the bar. A long gleaming mirror with frosted corners gave Drew a full view of the saloon.

No one out of the ordinary was there. Two cowboys played poker at a corner table. A whiskey bottle at the edge of the table was nearly empty.

In the opposite corner a drummer sat, a suitcase open on the table before him. He sipped a mug of beer while he sorted through his packets of buttons and spools of thread.

A black-haired saloon girl, wearing a green-and-yellow-striped knee-length taffeta dress with tiny straps over the shoulders leaned against the piano sipping something pink in a tall glass. The piano player, his blond hair slicked down tight against his scalp, ran his long fingers idly up and down the keys in no particular tune. He laughed up at the girl and she poked him in the shoulder.

Noticing Drew and Rick, she put the glass down on the tip of the piano and came toward them with springy steps. The smile on her olive-skinned face was real, not the artificial one girls of her profession usually wore. She didn't say anything until she'd gone behind the bar and stood in front of them.

"Gus had to go out for a while," she told them, a devilish sparkle in her big brown eyes. "So what can I get you?"

For a second Drew was taken aback by her genuine friendliness. He hadn't seen many friendly people lately.

"Two beers," he answered, pushing back his hat, "and maybe a little information."

"Coming right up," she said, spinning around in a flurry of skirt and petticoat. Turning the handle on the barrel spigot, she filled two mugs right up to the top, then set them carefully in front of the two thirsty men. In a couple of thirst-quenching gulps the mugs were empty, and they shoved the mugs across the bar for refills. With their thirst abated they took their time with these.

"What kind of information did you want?" she asked, turning sideways and leaning against the bar, resting her chin on her upturned palm. "I haven't been here very long, but since this is the only saloon in town, if you're looking for someone he'd most likely come in here."

"Well," Drew said, wiping the back of his hand across his mouth, "our luck will probably be the same here as in other places—all bad." He shook his head skeptically.

"Maybe not," she encouraged, smiling warmly and batting her eyes.

"We're looking for an old man," Drew began, expelling a long breath. "He's called a hider and smells like a dead buffalo."

A mischievous smile turned up the corners of her pink mouth. Then she clapped her hands together and her amused laughter filled the saloon.

"Mister, about half of the men who come in here smell like that." She cleared her throat and dabbed at the corner of her eyes with a dainty yellow handkerchief taken from the top of her dress. Drew and Rick exchanged questioning looks, then self-consciously glanced down at their own clothes. They each silently decided to take a bath later.

"If you'd seen this man, you'd never forget him," Drew went on, taking a leisurely sip and swallowing. "He's tall and thin. Walks a little slumped over and wears a big floppy black hat."

At each of the descriptions the girl shook her head, a doubtful expression in her blue eyes.

"He rides a mule," Rick put in slowly, lowering his head and watching the expression change on her face—change from doubt to wide-eyed excitement.

"Why didn't you tell me that in the first place," she chided, wagging her head from side to side and pressing her lips into a thin and annoyed line.

"You've seen him?" Drew asked, his brows arching hopefully.

"Oh, sure," she replied lightly, blinking her eyes. "He was in yesterday and early this morning." She paused a second, her entire face turning into a tight frown. "You know, you were right about one thing. I don't know what a dead buffalo smells like, but that old man had an odor you could smell all the way across the room. I'll bet he hadn't bathed in a month." Her nose wrinkled in disgust.

"Why didn't you recognize Caleb Dayton when we described him at first?" Drew asked, frowning across the bar at her.

"Mister, at least two thirds of the men who come in here could fit that description," she reflected in a level voice, her blue eyes flashing. "Not many men ride mules, you know. I saw him getting off his mule and coming in here yesterday morning when I was coming to work."

"What time was he in today?" Drew asked, a knot growing in his stomach. He realized he was wasting time here in the saloon asking questions of this exasperating girl. But he knew something final would happen today, and he also knew that he was trying to postpone the inevitable.

If Dayton killed him, Drew's pain and loss would be over. He took comfort in the fact that Rick would get Dayton, but then that would put a load of guilt on Rick and make him a part of something that was none of his doing. With that in mind, Drew told himself he had to be the one who stayed alive.

"I heard you asking about an old man riding a mule," a raspy voice said at Drew's right before the girl could answer. Drew looked up into the mirror to see who was talking. One of the cowboys who'd been playing poker was standing there, an empty glass dangling between a dirty-nailed finger and thumb. Drew knew whatever information he got out of the guy would cost him the price of a drink.

"Yeah," Drew answered. "I need to find him. Have you seen him?"

The cowboy's greenish-brown eyes sparkled at the thought of a lot of drinks. Drew knew exactly what he had in mind. "I'll buy you one drink," Drew said, his eyes narrowing and brows arching, "and I don't have a lot of time to waste."

The cowboy expelled a disgruntled snort and smacked his lips. "All right," he said, pushing his hat back. "I saw the old man about an hour ago." He dragged the words out in disappointment. He stopped and held out the glass. Drew nodded to the girl and she poured the glass full of whiskey. Before he said anything else the cowboy emptied the glass in one gulp.

"You were saying," Drew prompted. His voice was hard and his eyes were cold. "Where was he going?"

"He said his mule had thrown a shoe," the cowboy replied in a sullen voice, licking his lips. "He was going to have it fixed and ride on to Tucson."

Drew's blood ran cold. Tucson? Why would Dayton want to lead him all the way back to Tucson? Just to add insult to injury? They would have to go by Fort Rather, and that was just too much for Drew right now.

If the cowboy had seen Dayton only an hour ago, he'd probably be at the blacksmith shop right then.

"Let's go," Drew snapped sideways at Rick, slamming the beer mug down on the bar and spinning around on his heel.

"You've got to pay me first, mister," the girl reminded, holding out her hand and cocking her head to one side. She tapped her foot impatiently.

Drawing a fistful of coins from his pocket, Drew slapped them down on the bar. It didn't dawn on him that he'd left a half-full mug of beer there and that he'd overpaid for the drinks. Before the batwings had closed behind them, the cowboy had drained the mug and belched.

Since they hadn't passed a blacksmith shop on the way in, it stood to reason that it had to be at the opposite end of town.

Without waiting for Rick, Drew leaped into the saddle and, kicking the white horse in the side, raced down the street, stopping short when he saw the blacksmith's just ahead. A knot as large as his fist caught in his stomach and pulled at his lungs. His hands were sweating and his mouth was dry.

One of the largest black mules Drew had ever seen was standing tied to the hitch rail in front of the shop. The left back leg was bent and Drew could tell that it wasn't wearing a shoe. His own horse was tied to the right of the mule.

From inside he could hear the sounds of a hammer banging on metal. When the banging stopped, he heard the muffled voices of two men.

Rick pulled Money Man to a stop just as Drew dismounted at the side of the building and tied the white horse to a bush.

"Is Dayton inside?" Rick asked, moving up by Drew, easing the Colt .45 loose in the holster.

Drew nodded, stepping close to the wall. There was a slit between the planks and he peeped through. For a second the bulking figure of the smithy obscured most of the man Drew had been tracking for so long. Then the smithy moved over.

"Is that Dayton?" Drew asked Rick. He stepped aside so Rick could see. Rick peeped through the slit, stepped back, and nodded.

Drew resumed his place and looked closely at the man who'd caused him such misery. He was sitting on a nail keg, one long leg crossed over the other. The floppy black hat was pushed back on the shaggy brown hair streaked with gray. He looked ill-kept in a dirty blue shirt and black pants. Then Drew shifted his eyes back up to the old man's red-bearded face. The gaunt features looked tired. The thin mouth with a red mustache drooped at the corners and pulled a little to the left side.

For a split second Drew wanted to feel sorry for the old man. He was trying to vindicate his three sons' death just as Drew was doing with Melissa and the baby. The effort of so many days and so many miles was showing on the old hider.

But then Drew got a glimpse of Caleb Dayton's eyes. They were the coldest blue he'd ever seen. Hate and revenge had given them an icy glaze. There didn't seem to be any life in them at all. He turned his head to one side and spat a long stream of brown tobacco juice to the dirt floor. Then he wiped his shirt-sleeve across his mouth.

"How are you going to handle this?" Rick whispered close to Drew's shoulder. There was a tightness in his voice and his eyes were narrowed.

"By ear, I guess," Drew answered, adjusting his hat low over his eyes. This was it! The final showdown between him and Caleb Dayton!

Drawing his gun, he eased around the corner and up to the front of the shop and stopped. The smithy was hammering again. Dayton wouldn't be able to hear him, and he could shoot him in cold blood and it would all be over.

But, no! That wouldn't do. He wanted Dayton to know he was there and why he was there. A movement at his side caught his eye. Rick had drawn his gun and was advancing toward the door. From the frozen expression in Rick's eyes, Drew knew in an instant that he was going to save him a lot of trouble and kill Dayton himself.

That wasn't the way Drew wanted. He had to take care of it himself.

"Rick, no," he ordered in a whisper. "Stay out of this unless he gets me."

Rick glared at Drew but eased the gun halfway

down in the holster. He nodded, his mouth pulled tightly against his teeth.

Easing over behind a wagon with a broken wheel, Drew could see both Dayton and the smithy. Dayton had uncrossed his legs then recrossed them, and was leaning back against the wall as if he didn't have a care in the world. The smithy said something to Dayton and he laughed. A laughing sound came from Dayton's mouth but his eyes were full of hate, as was Drew's soul.

There was no point in waiting any longer. Drew wanted to get all of this over with. Moving away from the wagon's protection, Drew rested his hand on the butt of the pistol.

"Well, Dayton," he said slowly, "I've finally caught up with you. We've been almost to hell and back, but your time has finally run out. You're going to pay for what you did to my family."

Shock and disbelief narrowed Dayton's eyes, and for a second he sat as if glued to the keg. Then his blue eyes widened in momentary fear. Slowly a smirking grin pulled his thin mouth to one side and he arched a bushy brow.

"Williams, ye've got more trail savvy than I figured." Dayton's deep voice was cunning. There was also admiration in it. "I'd have give up long time ago if I was you. Did ye come to get me er yer horse?"

To Drew's dismay and irritation Dayton continued to sit on the keg. If he'd been in Dayton's boots, he'd have drawn a gun or at least looked for some kind of cover. That's what the smithy did. Apparently he'd seen enough call-outs and draw-downs in times past to know that some shooting was going to take place, and without saying a word had jumped back behind the open hearth and bellows. Drew was surprised that a man of such ponderous size could move so fast. He weighed at least three hundred pounds.

"I've got to know one thing," Drew said, his hand tightening on the handle of the still-holstered gun.

"What?" Dayton asked, uncrossing his legs and bringing the palms of his hands down on his knees.

"Why didn't you come after me first?" Drew asked coldly. "Why didn't you just come after me? Did you have to kill my wife and child?" He shook his head and his eyes were sad, but rage shook in his voice.

Cold hate snapped in Dayton's eyes. Slowly he moved his hands back and forth on his legs. He reminded Drew of a rattlesnake just about to strike.

"I'll tell ye exactly why I killed yer woman and kid," Dayton answered in a level voice, his steady gaze never leaving Drew's face. "Ye took what was mine so I did likewise."

Dayton's explanation made sense to only one person and that was Dayton.

"You won't believe this, Dayton," Drew said plaintively. "Slade was the only one of your sons that I actually killed, and that was in self-defense. You have only yourself to blame for what happened to your boys. They were giving guns to the Indians just like you are to Chihara. I was doing a job for the army when I . . ." A lump filled his throat when he thought about taking Melissa to Tucson. That had been his first meeting with the Daytons. ". . . went to Tucson. The Indians killed Cap, and the soldiers at Fort Rather killed Tom when he tried to escape. If you get lucky and get both me and Rick, are you going after the army and Chief Half Moon?"

He wanted to laugh at the smattering of sarcasm but didn't. It had no effect on Dayton anyway. He kept staring at Drew with the same hate-filled glare.

"Your sons were breaking the law," Drew shouted, "when I first met them. They were going to kidnap Melissa! She and the baby were innocent! You killed two innocent people because of your sons."

Suddenly Dayton leaned down to the right and behind him with a speed that surprised Drew, and jerked a rifle up by the barrel, swinging it against his side.

With a technique that Drew knew took a lot of practice, Dayton's gnarled fingers curled around the trigger and sent a bullet flying in his direction. With the same speed, Drew ducked behind a pile of wood just as the bullet whistled past his ear.

Starting to draw his pistol, Drew was distracted by a yell of pain to his right. From the corner of his eye Drew saw Rick bending over and grasping his thigh with both hands. Bright red blood was already staining his gray pants.

Drew's momentary lack of attention gave Dayton an unexpected break. Standing up with a fluidity that denied his age, Dayton leveled the rifle at Drew and, with enough hate in his eyes alone to kill a man, squeezed down on the trigger. Revenge and triumph pulled his mouth into a tight sneer.

But the almighty power that had taken care of Drew Williams all these years came through again. By some miraculous feat, the trigger jammed on Dayton's rifle and nothing happened.

Without wasting a second to question things, Drew

jumped up and rushed at Dayton. He had time to draw the Colt .45 and get this business over with. But that wouldn't do. That would be too easy.

Of course, Dayton wasn't about to stand there and let Drew take him without a fight. Throwing the rifle down with a curse and a grunt of disgust, Dayton quickly bent down and grabbed up a short piece of wood.

"Shoot him, Drew!" Rick's voice bellowed out in pain and dismay. "For God's sake. He'd do the same thing to you!"

This time Drew kept his attention on Dayton. The old hider started circling to his right, no doubt with the intention of getting outside. The door was behind and about ten feet from Drew.

Dayton would have to go around the hearth to get to the door, and if he did that Drew would lose him. But Drew still didn't want to shoot him.

Bending down, Drew made a low dive and caught Dayton around the knees, knocking him over backward. The air left Dayton's lungs in a rush and hiss. The impact of the fall dislodged the stick of wood from Dayton's hand, and for a second Drew thought the old man was defenseless. But that wasn't the case. Drew got the flashing image of a magician reaching into his bag of tricks when Dayton rolled to a squat and pulled a long, thin-bladed skinning knife from a sheath on his boot.

"He's going to kill you," Rick cautioned in a wild voice, "if you don't do something quick. What are you waiting for?"

A slow, confident grin pulled at Dayton's mouth. "Stay out of this," Dayton growled, bringing the knife up hip-level. "It ain't your fight." His words were for Rick, but his lowered gaze never left Drew's face.

The look in Dayton's eyes told Drew that he knew it was a two-man fight now and that there would be no shooting.

Dayton lunged at Drew, the blade reflecting the fire in the hearth. Drew stepped aside as the sharp blade barely missed him.

The smithy, knowing he had no part in this, other than that of an innocent bystander, had moved over to a corner, well out of the way, to watch the two men try to kill each other.

Drew had to get the knife away from Dayton. He could do a lot worse to Drew with that sharp knife than to a buffalo hide. He shivered at the sickening thought. Shifting his eyes rapidly around and overhead, the only thing that caught Drew's attention as a weapon was a length of trace chain about four feet long hanging from a nail on the right side of the wall. But a sawhorse stood in his way.

Dayton looked up at the same time and a different expression took shape in his eyes. The burning hate dimmed a degree and was replaced by that much fear.

The arm holding the knife dropped a little. Drew took advantage of the moment, and, as fast as he could, kicked the sawhorse out of the way, grabbed the chain, and jerked it and the nail from the wall.

Spinning around, Drew took a threatening swing at Dayton. The chain jangled as it swished through the air and swung Drew half way around with the momentum. For a split second Drew, feeling like a complete fool, questioned the merit of his action. He reached out as fast as he could so the falling chain wouldn't hit him on the legs.

Dayton threw back his shaggy head and roared in laughter. The fear had disappeared completely from his eyes and the hate eased back in.

"It's gonna be easy to kill ye, Williams," Dayton said slowly, gripping the knife handle hard. "Up until now ye haven't been this clumsy. I'm gonna cut ye up in little bitty pieces like wolf bait."

Drew's foolish feeling vanished at Dayton's criticism and the hot anger returned. Rage boiled in his stomach.

"I'm not finished with you yet, Dayton," Drew said in a low voice. He clenched his teeth together and a hard knot stood out in his jaw.

The blacksmith shop was blistering hot. Sweat oozed down Drew's face and into his eyes. He blinked the stinging away rapidly, never taking his gaze from Dayton's maniacal eyes. The part of Dayton's bearded face that Drew could see was also covered with sweat.

In Drew's earlier planning, it was going to be so simple to kill Dayton slowly. But now he realized it wasn't going to be so easy.

Dayton was far more adept with the knife he held so tightly in his hand than Drew was with the heavy and clumsy chain.

This wasn't the way it should be happening. He was supposed to have captured Dayton and slowly done away with him. Fate hadn't cooperated with him all that much.

"Are you going to stare at him the rest of the danged day?" Rick called out irritably. "Either you do something right now or I will."

At the sound of Rick's voice, Dayton dropped his guard and turned his head in that direction. Rick was standing at the door, the light behind him. The bright sunlight affected Dayton's vision, and he blinked his eyes and frowned.

Drew knew that fate was taking care of him again and he quickly took advantage of the opportunity.

Drawing back his arm and gripping the chain tightly, Drew leaped across the short distance. Swinging the chain before Dayton's eyes could focus, Drew was shocked when the metal wrapped around Dayton's arm, the force knocking the knife from his hand. The knife landed with a thud in the sand a few feet away from Dayton.

Fortified with the fact that Dayton was disarmed, Drew jerked on the chain and pulled Dayton toward him. Switching the chain to his left hand, Drew pulled his right arm back and hit Dayton as hard as he could with his fist.

The blow caught Dayton on the chin and he staggered back. He looked like a circus clown as he tried to no avail to regain his balance.

When Drew had pulled Dayton toward him and switched hands, the chain had slackened a little and fell from Dayton's arm. Drew looked quickly from the dangling chain to the prone man on the dirt floor.

"Well, Dayton," Drew said coldly, taking a threatening step toward the man who'd led him on a wild chase for days, "now who's going to take who?"

Drew thought that Dayton would make some kind of plea for his life or at least make a bargain with his. But that wasn't the case. Dayton just stared up at him. The passiveness in Dayton's cold eyes angered

Drew to the core.

"Get up," Drew shouted, his mouth drawn tightly against his teeth. "Get up, damn you! Get up and fight me like a man! I'm sure my wife put up more of a struggle than you are." Dayton still didn't move. He just continued lying on the ground and looking up at Drew. "Get up, I said," Drew's eyes were blazing and his face was almost purple in rage.

"Mister, why don't you drop this thing?" The voice belonged to the blacksmith. He'd finally come out from his hiding place and held a rifle in his big dirty hands.

The rifle, looking like a toy in the smithy's hands, wasn't aimed at anyone, and Drew had the feeling that it was only to give the man some much-needed courage. "Whatever wrong he done you—and I take it that he killed your woman and kid—could be handled by the sheriff. Why don't you let your friend go and get him. He could also see the doc about his leg. I'll hold my gun on Dayton there."

He nodded his head toward Dayton, who had pulled himself into a sitting position on the ground. Drew glanced over at Rick who was leaning against the doorjamb. His face was pale and the top part of his pants leg was soaked in blood, the stain creeping down.

Drew didn't want Rick to suffer any more on his account, and nodded in agreement to part of the smithy's suggestion.

"That's a good idea," Drew said, cocking an eyebrow, a plan taking shape in his mind. There was no reason for Rick to be a party to the rest of this. Turning all the way around he faced his cousin, a smile, just a small one, on his lips. "Rick, go find the sheriff. Tell him to get down here on the double, and then find a doctor to patch up your leg. I'll see you later at the saloon."

From the look in Drew's eyes, Rick knew without a doubt that as soon as he was gone, trouble was going to break out again. Drew hadn't chased Dayton all over the country for nothing, and wasn't about to give him up to a sheriff. Anything could happen, even if Dayton did end up in jail.

Knowing how bad Drew's shoulder must have hurt when the rock had been lodged in it, Rick, with the bullet still in his leg, nodded, turned, and started hobbling away. He paused for a second and looked back over his shoulder at Drew, a knowing in his eyes.

"I'll see you later," he said, narrowing his eyes. "I remember what I promised you."

Drew knew that Dayton wouldn't make it to jail even if Rick did send the sheriff to the blacksmith shop.

Hearing a sound behind him, Drew turned to see Dayton getting to his feet, a smug smile on his bearded face.

Drew still had the chain in his left hand but switched it back again to the right.

"So," Dayton said, a sneer in his gravelly voice, "the smart wagon scout is puttin' his tail between his legs and givin' up, eh." Dayton threw back his head and laughed.

"No, I'm not giving up," Drew answered, his voice rising and his mouth tightening. "Rick's been through enough because of you and me. He needed a doctor."

The smithy stepped back a few paces, still holding

the rifle. But it wasn't aimed at anyone. In fact, the barrel was almost touching the dirt floor.

"You don't have the guts, Williams," Dayton taunted, a challenge in his narrowing eyes. "You're too much of a coward."

Drew couldn't understand why Dayton was trying to get him riled. Did he actually want Drew to kill him?

Drew had never been called a coward by anyone, and the fact that he'd tracked Dayton for so long should have been proof against that. But the accusation sent a sheet of rage all over Drew, and he felt like he was on fire and would explode.

Without thinking or planning, he tightened his grip on the chain and swung it as hard as he could. If he hadn't had his body braced against the force, he would have lost his balance and fallen. But not so this time. The chain swished through the air, and the curse and yell of pain from Dayton told Drew that the chain had found its mark.

A thrill that almost equalled sexual ecstacy shot through Drew at the sight of a deep cut visible on Dayton's left cheek.

Dayton reached up with his left hand and winced in agony when he touched his bleeding face. His eyes blazed when he lowered his hand and saw that it was covered with blood.

"I should have killed ye that first night on the trail," Dayton roared, glancing wildly around the blacksmith shop. If he was looking for a weapon or help from the smithy, he found neither.

The smithy stood watching the two men, his already-wide eyes popping out, the gun he was holding forgotten. The barrel was sunken in the dirt floor.

"It wouldn't have helped you," Drew told him through clenched teeth. "If you had been lucky and got me, it wouldn't have done you any good. Rick promised me, just as I swore on Melissa's grave, that you would die."

Certainty gleamed in Drew's hard eyes. He was breathing hard.

"Why don't ye jest let the sheriff have me?" Dayton asked, a cunning in his eyes that reminded Drew of a fox. "I'll be tried and no doubt hung. Ye won't have my death on your hands."

So! Dayton was finally begging for his sorry life. It sickened Drew. He was sure that Dayton would go down for the count. Or was Dayton baiting him again?

Drew blinked his eyes, and in that time Dayton made a dive for the forgotten rifle the blacksmith was holding. His own rifle was too far away for him to reach.

But age and fate were working against Dayton and for Drew. Bending low, Drew swung the chain again. His aim was as accurate this time as before. The chain caught Dayton around the ankles, bringing him down on his stomach with a grunt. When he rolled over on his back, fear was rampant in his eyes.

"Get up!" Drew said, soft but deadly. Hatred changed his features into those of a madman. "Pretend that I'm Melissa. Did she plead for her life and the baby's life like you're doing? Did she beg you not to hurt her? Did she even know who you were? Answer me!"

Drew's shouts bounced off the wall and rang in his

ears. The questions put an uncontrollable rage in him, and before he realized it he'd drawn back the chain and smashed it down across Dayton's shoulders. The sharp cracking of Dayton's left shoulder bone was mixed with his yell of pain.

"I don't know if she knew who I was," Dayton whimpered, reaching up with his right hand to touch his shattered shoulder. "I meant to kill ye for what ye done to my boys. But ye wasn't there. She was second best."

All of Dayton's bravado was gone. All of his cunning had disappeared when he realized that he was at Drew's mercy. He was just a pitiful-looking broken mess cringing on the ground.

Something snapped in Drew when Dayton said that Melissa and the baby had been used as a substitute for him, and all reasoning of right and wrong vanished from his mind.

Melissa was the best thing that had ever happened to him, and he'd known that when the baby was born his life would be complete.

All of that had changed when a worthless piece of humanity had tried to avenge the law-sanctioned death of his cutthroat sons.

He had no authority to bring Dayton in. What he was doing now was as much against the law as anything the four Daytons had ever done. But he was certain that if he turned Dayton over to the sheriff, the wheels of justice would turn much too slowly for his peace of mind. Dayton's fate was still up to him.

"The sheriff should be here any second," the blacksmith said uncertainly, an expression of horror and disbelief all over his ruddy face. Even if the sheriff didn't come, he wasn't going to take sides in this. From the look in the young man's eyes he'd kill anyone who got in his way.

Drew knew the sheriff wouldn't be coming right away, if at all, and the smithy's words just barely penetrated his hate-clouded brain.

Before he realized what he was doing, Drew had drawn back his arm and brought the chain down across Dayton's sagging back just below his neck. The buffalo hider pitched forward and lay moaning, his face almost buried in the sand. The gnarled fingers on his right hand clawed four grooves in the sand. A mental picture of Melissa trying to protect her stomach and then lying helpless flashed before Drew's eyes. He seemed to step outside himself, and he couldn't believe what he was seeing himself do!

The arm holding the chain was brought back again and again. It swished through the air again and again at an object just above something that resembled a man's shoulders, and he could hear bones cracking.

But a man's head was supposed to be atop his shoulders, Drew tried to reason. No one could possibly describe the bloody pulp on the ground as a head. It looked like a red melon that had been trampled on by a horse. The body on the ground didn't move or make a sound. A deep red color was being absorbed into the dirt.

From far away Drew could hear the blacksmith's voice calling to him. Anguish was in his voice.

"Mister, stop it! You've already killed him! The man's as dead as he's going to be. Stop it or I'll shoot you!"

Drew's gaze slowly focused on the smithy, but it

took a little while for him to collect himself. When he did, he looked slowly down at the end of the chain. It was red and matted with strands of hair, blood, and pieces of bone. Drew felt sick when it dawned on him that the bone was Dayton's skull! Or what was left of it.

Looking down at the bloody heap on the floor, Drew got sick to his stomach. Whirling around, he ran to an empty corner and vomited up a bitter-tasting mass of hatred and revenge.

Straightening up, he wiped his face with a handkerchief then threw it on the floor. Hurrying over to the water bucket the smithy used to cool horseshoes, Drew stuck his head down in the metallic-smelling water and kept it there until his lungs began hurting and he was sure he'd drown.

Standing up slowly, he pushing his dripping-wet hair back from his eyes and turned to face the blacksmith, who looked as sick as Drew had just been. His face was pale and his thick lips trembled.

"I don't want any trouble, mister," he said fearfully, jerking up the rifle and aiming it at Drew. Shaking his head slowly, Drew stared at the smithy.

"I just beat a man to death with a trace chain," Drew muttered in disbelief, a wild look in his eyes. Shaking his head slowly, he swallowed hard. "It took me a long time to get my revenge on him and it doesn't feel the way it should."

Drew felt empty inside. Dayton was dead. He'd paid for what he'd done to Melissa and Little Moon. Drew was still alone and would be for a long time. Why didn't he feel good about this?

What was before him? What would he do? Where

would he go? He would become the hunted man.

Turning abruptly on his heel, he walked out the door, not really surprised to see Rick come limping down the street alone. Drew had known that Rick wouldn't get the sheriff.

Drew was surprised, though, that there weren't some people outside. The commotion inside the blacksmith shop hadn't been all that quiet. The shot should have attracted someone. But apparently a shot was a common thing here in Carmen.

"What do we do now?" Rick asked, watching Drew intently.

Glancing down at his boots for a second, Drew raised his head and looked at Rick from the corner of his eyes.

"I guess we'd better go tell the sheriff what happened in there," Drew said laconically and nodding toward the blacksmith shop. He untied his horse, then he and Rick went around to the side of the shop for the other horses.

"How do you feel?" Rick asked, catching up the horse's reins.

"Not the way I thought I would," Drew answered sorrowfully, mounting up on the white horse and leading his. Rick swung up on Money Man. "Dayton is dead. I killed him in cold-blooded revenge. That makes me no better than him."

They were halfway down the street when a strange expression crossed Drew's face.

"I'm not going to give myself up right now," he said, narrowing his eyes, a puzzling smile on his mouth. He kicked the white horse in the side and they rode at a fast gallop down the street in the opposite direction they'd just come. There was no sign of the smithy when they rode by the blacksmith shop.

At the edge of town Drew pulled the white horse to a stop. "Well," he said shrewdly, a tight smile on his face. He reached over and slapped Rick on the shoulder. "Here's where we part company. I'm sure a posse will be coming after me as soon as the smithy tells the sheriff what happened back there. There's no point in you being caught up in any more of this. The Barbary Coast is waiting for you."

"What's waiting for you?" Rick asked, smiling wanly at him.

"I think I'll go back to Mexico for a while," Drew replied almost sadly, taking and expelling a deep breath. "They can't bother me there." He straightened in the saddle, throwing back his shoulders.

"Good luck, Drew," Rick said, sympathy in his voice. He extended his hand.

"You, too, Rick," Drew said, gripping his hand in a firm shake.

Without saying anything else, Rick reined Money Man around to the right and headed west. Pulling Nino Blanco to the left, and with a load of guilt on his shoulders, Drew headed south to the border.

THE UNTAMED WEST
brought to you by Zebra Books

THE LAST MOUNTAIN MAN (1480, $2.25)
by William W. Johnstone
He rode out West looking for the men who murdered his father and brother. When an old mountain man taught him how to kill a man a hundred different ways from Sunday, he knew he'd make sure they all remembered . . . THE LAST MOUNTAIN MAN.

SAN LOMAH SHOOTOUT (1853, $2.50)
by Doyle Trent
Jim Kinslow didn't even own a gun, but a group of hardcases tried to turn him into buzzard meat. There was only one way to find out why anybody would want to stretch his hide out to dry, and that was to strap on a borrowed six-gun and ride to death or glory.

TOMBSTONE LODE (1915, $2.95)
by Doyle Trent
When the Josey mine caved in on Buckshot Dobbs, he left behind a rich vein of Colorado gold—but no will. James Alexander, hired to investigate Buckshot's self-proclaimed blood relations learns too soon that he has one more chance to solve the mystery and save his skin or become another victim of TOMBSTONE LODE.

GALLOWS RIDERS (1934, $2.50)
by Mark K. Roberts
When Stark and his killer-dogs reached Colby, all it took was a little muscle and some well-placed slugs to run roughshod over the small town—until the avenging stranger stepped out of the shadows for one last bloody showdown.

DEVIL WIRE (1937, $2.50)
by Cameron Judd
They came by night, striking terror into the hearts of the settlers. The message was clear: Get rid of the devil wire or the land would turn red with fencestringer blood. It was the beginning of a brutal range war.

Available wherever paperbacks are sold, or order direct from the Publisher. Send cover price plus 50¢ per copy for mailing and handling to Zebra Books, Dept. 2016, 475 Park Avenue South, New York, N.Y. 10016. Residents of New York, New Jersey and Pennsylvania must include sales tax. DO NOT SEND CASH.